JAQ

Also by Ronan Bennett

Fiction

The Second Prison

Overthrown by Strangers

The Catastrophist

Havoc, in its Third Year

Zugzwang

Non-fiction

Stolen Years: Before and After Guildford

Fire and Rain: Life and Death in Long Kesh

Double Jeopardy: The Retrial of the Guildford Four

Film

Public Enemies

The Hamburg Cell

Face

A Further Gesture

Television

Top Boy

Gunpowder

10 Days to War

Hidden

Rebel Heart

A Man You Don't Meet Every Day

JAQ

A *TOP BOY* STORY

RONAN BENNETT

HARPERVIA

An Imprint of HarperCollins*Publishers*

First HarperVia edition published 2024

FIRST EDITION

Library of Congress Cataloging-in-Publication Data has been applied for.

ISBN 978-0-06-333793-0

23 24 25 26 27 LBC 5 4 3 2 1

To Molly and Finn
and
Georgina, always

DUSHANE, SULLY AND ME

Everyone knows I rolled with Dushane and Sully and the Summerhouse mandem. That's out there. Ain't no secret.

And by now, most people think they know how it all ended. Maybe they do. Or also maybe they don't. Or they know bits of it and that makes them think they know the whole story.

They don't.

But I do, and, trust me, there's way more to it than what people think they know. And I'm going to tell you everything. I'm gonna tell you the whole story, including details you have no idea about. And when you've heard it, you'll understand why it went down the way it did.

Of the two of them, Sully and Dushane, I clicked way better with Sully. Dushane never really had mandem round him like that, you know? Dushane never had no friends. He had calm eyes. But when he looked at people, if you looked close, you could see, even if he was smiling, you could see him thinking is this person gonna be useful to me? It was always a calculation with Dushane. If he decided yeah, I can use this fella or this girl, then he might be nice to your face. He'd give you all his bullshit. Like he gave Ra'Nell way back in the day. He talent-spotted Ra'Nell, innit. But he was never friends with Ra'Nell. Never.

Here's the difference. I'm talking about Sully now. Sully had friends. He didn't have a lotta friends because Sully was actually a shy man. I'm serious. Bad man Summerhouse Sully was actually shy man Sully. But if Sully liked you, he would take care of you. Like he done with Jason. Jason was like the dumbest kid. Jason used to literally sleep in wheelie bins. He never washed. He never changed his clothes. He stank. That's the kind of life he come from because his mum was a proper nittie.

I don't like calling people losers because, depending what day it is, you might be winning or losing, and tomorrow it might be a whole different situation. But Jason was a loser. Sorry, but there ain't no other way to put it. Tomorrow wasn't gonna be no different for Jason. And not the day after, or the day after that. Nah. Jason was gonna be a loser his whole life. Which, in the end, weren't that long.

But still, Sully looked after Jason. He tried to keep Jason safe. I saw the man after Jason got torched in that house down in Ramsgate. It hit Sully hard. I mean, really hard. You'd see Sully sniffing his hands. He'd be sitting there normal and then he lifts his hands to his face and sniffs them. The reason he done that? He was convinced he could still smell the smoke from the fire that killed Jason. Even weeks later, he swore he could smell it. I think what he smelt was his own guilt cos I believe Sully blamed himself. But it weren't his fault what happened to Jason. A bunch of racists came and firebombed the house cos there were immigrants living there and Jason just happened to be there too. Wrong place, wrong time.

That's the difference between Sully and Dushane. Dushane didn't care about no one, but he pretended he did. Sully cared, but he pretended he didn't. I never trusted Dushane. But Sully was different. I liked the man. I liked the way he carried himself. When I looked in Sully's eyes, they were deep. You could see there was a person in there who wasn't happy with the way he actually was. You never saw much joy. But he was trying. Sully was doing work on himself. Like I was. Like I am still, you could say.

I don't want you to get the wrong idea when I say this, but . . . all right, I'm just gonna put this out there . . . I loved the man. All right, I said it. Now, when I say I loved him, I don't mean I had them kind of feelings for him. You know the kind I'm talking about. Cos, trust me, there ain't never been a time when I had them kind of feelings for boys. It's always been girls for me. But I loved Sully.

I know exactly what you're thinking. You're saying to yourself this girl is full of shit. Cos you all think you know what happened. You're saying to yourself, funny kind of love considering what went down. I hear you. But you're wrong. I loved the man.

The road is like that. You never know where it's gonna take you. You take your first step and you might think you know where you're going. But you don't. No one does, and anyone who tries to tell you different, that they're in control, they know what they're doing, that person's just full of shit. On the road, all you can do is keep putting one foot in front of the other and then wait and see what happens next. If you're lucky, you keep moving more or less in the direction you think you wanna go. If luck ain't on your side, anything can happen. Shit you never in your life thought could ever happen.

The morning after the Summerhouse riot – that was a madness – that morning I knew Sully would wanna talk and that talk was gonna be difficult for me. Either way I was in the worst kind of situation, the kind where it looks like you've got options but the reality is you don't cos no matter what you do you know things are gonna get messy.

Nothing worse than being in that situation. Am I right?

You all think you know what happened next. But this is the true story behind what you think you know.

GIRLS' NIGHT OUT

Depending how far back you want to go in the whole history of the Summerhouse mandem, you could say it all started way back in the times of Bobby Raikes and Lee Greene. That was a long time ago, when Dushane and Sully were just starting out and I was just a girl still at school. I wasn't on the road then, but I've heard plenty of people talking since. Bits and pieces. Enough to know that that's when the bad blood started between them two. And over the years it just built up and got worse, even when they were working together and making a lot of Ps for each other.

But I don't wanna go back to them times. It's not necessary cos as far as I'm concerned it was the night I was in Chasers when the whole thing kicked off.

Chasers is this dodgy club in the West End that for some reason Becks likes. I never liked it that much. I'm there cos Becks wanted to go with her posh friends to celebrate one of their birthdays and also one of them got promotion at work.

They'd already had a few drinks by the time I arrive.

Someone pours me a glass of champagne and this girl who's got the promotion, Lucia, says to me how happy Becks is.

'We've all been really worried about her,' she says. 'The last girl Becks was with was a nightmare. She was so needy. It was all about her, her, her. She made Becks miserable. But since she got together with you, she's been so happy.'

'I'm happy too,' I say. Which is true.

'You make a great-looking couple,' she says. 'What do you do?'

I'm not sure exactly what she's asking.

'For work, I mean?' she says.

'I ain't really working right now,' I tell her.

'OK,' she says, with a little bit of an edge which I don't care for.

Her girlfriend Sharon comes over and kisses me on both cheeks. I've met Sharon a couple of times before, but she's not a friend of mine by any means. Sharon's a little drunk and very smiley.

She says, 'Jaq, you must know someone who could get us some office supplies.'

I've heard it called a thousand different things, but I've never heard it called office supplies before. But of course I know what she's talking about.

'Just to keep the party going,' Lucia says with a big grin.

OK, two things about this.

First off, along with Becks, I'm the only Black girl in their company and she comes to ask me. Maybe that ain't so surprising. A lotta people assume if you're Black, you can get them drugs.

But second, Sharon is a fed.

Maybe that ain't so surprising either. Because the more

you find out about the Metropolitan Police these days, the more they look like just another London gang. And anyway, feds are people like the rest of us. They do what the rest of us do. And a lot of us like to get high.

Sharon's smiling this big smile at me. 'Go on,' she says.

So I say, 'Yeah, maybe. Lemme see.'

'That would be amazing,' Sharon says and she kisses me again.

So I send Kieron a wassap saying bring some white, some E and some MDMA. Bring the good stuff.

Kieron's my guy. Him and Romy both, but really Kieron. He's family. He would do anything for me, and sure enough less than an hour later he's outside the club with the order. I slip it to Sharon and she goes back inside with Lucia.

Then something weird happens. Kieron's phone and my phone start pinging like there's a million people wanting to talk to us. The same million.

We look at our phones. There's bare messages. They're still coming in.

'Fuck me. What?'

We both say the same words at the same time. And then we look at each other.

'Fuck me,' is all I can say. 'I mean, fuck me. Is this for real?'

On the road, news travels very fast. It has to. Say the bando gets robbed. Or say someone gets shot or stabbed up somewhere. Well, obvious, you gotta know about it quick cos next it could be you. You have to be on it the whole time. Plus, truth is the mandem like to gossip. They like their war stories. And, fuck me, is this a war story.

Someone had just switched off Jamie Tovell.

Jamie Tovell who took over the Fields mandem from

Modie and then had this big idea he liked to call Zero Tolerance where he was going to unite all the gangs so there wouldn't be no more wars. Jamie who threw Cam off a high rise. Jamie who tried to lay out Dushane and Sully.

Jamie has just been shot dead.

That's a fucking war story.

I look at Kieron and I just say, 'What the fuck?'

I'm in shock. He's in shock.

My first thought, can't lie, is I could get the blame for this. Cos it was well known that me and Jamie did not get on. I never liked man. And he never liked me. So I'm thinking, Dushane's gonna blame me for this. Even though it weren't me. I mean, I've been here the whole time with the girls. But Dushane ain't gonna believe these girls. They're white and posh. Why would he believe them?

'Who done him?' I ask Kieron.

I know he don't know any more than me, but I wanna know what he's thinking. Kieron shrugs. But the look he gives me tells me he's thinking along the same lines I'm thinking.

I quickly text Dushane with the news. He don't answer me back.

I don't want Kieron to go cos when you get big news like this you want to have one of your own around, just to talk with and share your feelings and feel safe. Someone who knows who you are and understands you. And all I have is Sharon the fed, Lucia who says she's in 'medical consultancy' whatever the fuck that is, another girl whose name I can never remember who works for Vivienne Westwood, which is cool, but I'm not on the same wave-length as this girl, and another girl who works for Transport for London. Them kind of people. Not exactly my people.

But Kieron has to go. His mum Diana is very bad with

cancer and has been having more chemo which is making her very sick and he don't like her being alone.

'Text me if you hear anything more,' I say, and we fist bump and then I hug him.

Kieron's a quiet fella, but he's solid. I mean physically – he's thin but all muscle, if you get me. But I also mean mentally. He never loses his temper, not like me. And he's a good judge of people. If there's someone Kieron don't trust, you know that person ain't worth trusting. I always like having Kieron around. But he has to leave.

I go back inside. Becks smiles like a naughty girl and bites into an E and she takes half and holds out the other half for me. I'm thinking I shouldn't cos after this Jamie thing who knows what shit is gonna go down. I need to be on it. But I look at Becks and I just wanna be in the same space where she is. You should be able to get off your face when you want. Except maybe this weren't probably the best time, cos of the Jamie thing. There's gonna be comeback on that. Hundred per cent.

I take the half tab and Becks gives me a bottle of water to sip. I know I'm gonna regret this cos when I get high – especially when there's champagne involved – the next two days I'm dead. I mean literally dead.

That half a tab is only the start. I dance. I sing. I snog Becks. I flirt. I laugh. I do a couple of lines to keep the energy levels up. I take a whole tab of MDMA. I drink more champagne. I drink some shots. At least I think I've got a memory of some shots.

Me and Becks get back to mine about six in the morning. I totally forget to look at my phone.

I wake up at two o'clock in the afternoon and I'm feeling way worse even than I thought I would. Then I remember.

Jamie.

I sit bolt upright in bed. Becks doesn't move. That girl can sleep. If there was an Olympics for sleeping, she would win every medal going. I crawl out of bed. I mean, I'm literally crawling on my hands and knees. I get to the kitchen. I'm so dehydrated. I drink water. I drink some juice. Then I call Kieron.

I gotta work out how this is gonna affect me. Cos situations like this, they can escalate very easy.

THIS SO-CALLED MYSTERIOUS FIGURE

On the road, you never get the full story all in one go. It comes in bits and pieces. And it's never a hundred per cent reliable. Someone says one thing, it sounds about right, but then someone else says something else that is the total opposite of what you've just heard but it sounds right too. Out in the straight world, the straight people have what they call their paper of record. I overheard Becks call it that when she was talking on the phone to one of her marketing clients. Paper of record. But Becks told me that even the paper of record ain't always reliable. There's always another point of view, always someone telling you different. So just imagine what it's like for us on the road. We don't have no paper of record. Instead, you've got a hundred different people telling you a hundred different stories and you've gotta work out what's true and what ain't.

It's a fucking headache, I can't lie.

The first version of what went down, I heard this way.

Jamie was in his yard with his brothers, eating dinner. Someone come to the door and I don't know why but

Jamie opened up. I mean, why would man do that? Someone like Jamie, he had enemies. We all have enemies. I have enemies. And you don't open the door easy. You know what I'm saying?

Maybe Jamie looked out the spyhole and whoever it was he weren't worried. Or maybe he was expecting somebody and assumed it was them. Or maybe he was so relaxed or high or happy he didn't look out the spyhole the way he should. If he didn't, he should of cos whoever come that night had a strap in his hand and he shot Jamie point blank.

The way I heard, when Jamie was on the floor the two brothers come running out. They saw the fella, whoever it was . . . well, now we all know who it was but, on the road, even when something is known for a fact, you kind of never say the name. Or at least you never should. That's just the way it is. So you're always careful about saying names out loud.

Anyway, the brothers, they saw who it was and they saw him lean over Jamie and shoot him in the head, just to make sure.

Then this so-called mysterious figure, who actually ain't so mysterious at all, turns and goes. And the brothers are screaming and crying.

That's a fucking war story.

But there's more. And this is what really blew my mind.

Jamie getting laid out weren't that big a surprise. Jamie was a roadman. People on the road, they get shot in the head. It happens. People talk about it for a while, but actually nothing much changes. Somebody might get shot or stabbed in retaliation, but the big wheels of life will just keep turning.

But this next part was fucking un-fucking-believable. This was gonna change everything. And it meant no one could be sure where they stood. Including me.

I'm in the kitchen with the worst hangover anyone has ever had. My jaw hurts and I keep needing the toilet and bits and pieces of the story are coming in, probably not even half of it true. But slowly I'm putting a picture together. And it's scary.

I call Kieron. 'Bruv, what are you hearing about Dushane and Sully?'

'It's fucked up,' he says.

'Bruv! Is it true?'

'I'm coming over to yours,' he says.

He don't wanna talk on the phone. He don't wanna say names out loud. I go to the toilet again and by the time I'm done, Kieron's at the door.

We sprawl out on the sofa. Or I sprawl and he sits.

'What I'm hearing,' he says, 'is Shelley and Dushane were at this posh place last night having dinner. Shelley's talking to him about this plan she has to build up her nail bar business.'

'Yeah, I heard she's got her eye on some chain or something she wants to buy.'

'Yeah, from this Vietnamese lady Kim. Then, hear this, Dushane's in the toilets and who comes in behind him?'

'Sully?'

'Sully.'

I guessed right. 'Fuck me.'

'This is like less than an hour after Jamie got laid out.'

'Fuck me.'

'So around the time I saw you at the club.'

My head can't take this in.

'And then they're in the toilets and Sully sticks a strap in Dushane's face.'

'I don't believe this shit.'

'And Sully puts it to him. Either Dushane steps back from the business or bang, it's all over.'

'What did Dushane say?'

'Dushane's still alive so I'm assuming that must mean he swallowed it.'

'What?!'

Dushane's stepping back? Dushane ain't top boy no more?

'Think about it, Jaq,' Kieron says. 'Dushane ain't got much choice, cos let's face it, who are the mandem gonna roll with? It ain't gonna be Dushane, is it?'

Kieron's right about that. The old Dushane was good not just at talent-spotting. He knew how to put a team together and how to get the best out of them. And he knew how to keep a team together, keep them happy. He used to know all their names, their brothers' names, their mums' names, and he'd call them by their names, which made them feel valued. He knew all their problems, which made them feel he cared. He didn't, but they thought he did.

But the more money Dushane made, the less time he spent with the team. He doesn't know half their names now. He doesn't even pretend to care about them. All he cares about is that they sell his food and bring him the correct money back.

So the soldiers out there on their corners in all weathers, all hours of the day and night, looking out for feds and rival gangsters, running all the risks, they stop having feelings of loyalty for him. They don't like him cos he never gives them any reason to like him.

I'm not saying the soldiers like Sully. But they respect Sully cos Sully is never afraid to get his hands dirty, you get me? Dushane is more management. Distant. Sully is the groundsman. He works on the floor. And work on the floor sometimes means pulling the trigger. Everyone knows Sully's pulled the trigger, even if there ain't no proof, cos with the good criminal mind Sully has, he ain't gonna do that kind of work where there's cameras. He ain't gonna leave behind no prints or DNA.

'Sully's making a play,' Kieron says. 'First, he switched off Jamie, which he knew Dushane wouldn't like so he had to make his move on Dushane quick so there wouldn't be no comeback.'

It was Sully pulled the trigger on Jamie. I know in my bones it was him. I feel like shit. We have a lot to talk about, but right now my head is banging. Hangover is bad enough and there's just too much information spinning around. I tell Kieron I need to get back to bed and he goes.

But before I undertake that long, hard journey from the kitchen to the bedroom, I take another quick look at my messages. I'm thinking there's gonna be one from Sully because sooner or later there definitely will be. But there's no message from him. Not yet.

Instead, there's a text from a number I don't recognise. Normally, I wouldn't open a message from a number I don't know, but because of everything that's happened, I open it.

It's from fucking Sharon.

Sharon the fucking fed.

I mean, what the fuck?

I don't even remember giving Sharon my number. Or

maybe I did. Or maybe it was Becks or one of the other girls. Anyway there's a message.

Sharon wants to meet, just her and me.

Fuck me. I mean, seriously, fuck me. What does this girl wanna talk about?

A fucking fed wants to talk, just her and me. The day after Jamie gets laid out? For all I know, maybe she's thinking she can get some information from me. Solve the murder. That would make her look good in the eyes of her Metropolitan Police gangster bosses. I don't like this at all, I can't lie.

I sip some more water and somehow I make that trek back to the bedroom. Climbing Everest would be easier.

'Becks,' I say. 'Wake up, I want a cuddle.'

But Becks is in one of her Olympic marathon sleeps. She is not gonna wake up and I can't get back to sleep.

The whole world has just got turned upside down.

LAURYN

You're thinking my day could not get any worse. That's what I'm thinking. It couldn't get worse.

But it does.

Cos there's someone I ain't mentioned yet. Lauryn.

I love my sister. I do. But she is a fully loaded headache. And I don't even feel guilty saying that about my own sister. The girl just attracts drama. And it's always drama she can't deal with so she puts it on me. The number of times I have had to clean up her shit. And she's the older one. But it's what we do, innit. We ride out for family.

I'm telling you, being born beautiful actually doesn't do a girl any favours. I mean, I'm beautiful, I'm very beautiful. And so is Becks. Becks is stunning. But Lauryn is a different kind of beautiful. From when she was a little baby, everyone kept telling her what a beautiful girl she was.

So it ain't no surprise she grew up thinking she was special and all she had to do was be beautiful and she'd get whatever she wanted. And if she got in trouble all she would have to do is smile and bat her eyelids and people would say, nah, don't worry about it, beautiful.

Fuck me, that girl has caused me so much problems. At school, the other girls could be little bitches. They were jealous of her, innit, and they'd pick on her. And who had to sort it out? One time, I was in Year 11, this girl Kendra was in the corridor outside the library slapping and kicking Lauryn and pulling her hair. I jumped in and I proper battered Kendra and told her and her friends that if they ever touched Lauryn again I would kill them. They knew I meant it. Lauryn never had no more problems from that quarter ever again, trust me.

But maybe I should of let Lauryn sort out her own problems. Cos Lauryn grew up thinking if anything went bad she could just come to me and go, 'Jackie, Jackie, help me.' Like she done after she nearly got Sully killed that time when he was on his way to Jason's cremation cos of her loose pillow talk with one of the opps and she had to leave Summerhouse and go and live in Liverpool where she ended up with that nutter Curtis. That was a whole different level of drama.

I ain't gonna talk here about how that particular problem of Curtis got solved. Like I said, on the road there are certain things you shouldn't go into the details of and you shouldn't name names, although sometimes you can get a bit careless and you do. But you shouldn't, even when the dogs in the street know every name there is to know and exactly who done what.

But you already know Curtis ain't around no more. And on the road, if you say there's a beef between two people and then you say one of them ain't around no more, what that means that person probably ain't gonna be seen around no more. So I'll say it again. Curtis ain't around no more.

I can't lie, with Lauryn it's complicated.

For a start, since Lauryn came home she ain't got nowhere of her own to live. She could go back to Mum's, I suppose, except she don't wanna live there cos of what happened with Curtis and also because Mum is even more of a liability than Lauryn. So Lauryn has been staying mostly at mine.

I'm just starting to fall asleep when someone starts shaking me, saying, 'Wake up, wake up.'

I'm thinking it's Becks, but it ain't. I look at Lauryn although my eyes ain't focusing right.

'What?'

'Jackie, Jackie,' she says. 'It's the baby.'

Now I'm alert. 'What's wrong with the baby?'

'He's kicking. He won't stop.'

That's all?

Lauryn's eyes are all swollen from crying. She's practically dragging me out the bed. 'Jackie, Jackie.'

I can feel Becks' hand sliding off my shoulder.

'What time is it?' Becks says without opening her eyes.

I ain't got no idea, do I. I stumble out after Lauryn as Becks turns over and goes back to sleep. How I wish that was me.

In the kitchen, Lauryn starts crying her eyes out.

'I can't have this baby,' she says.

'Lauryn. It's way too late to do anything about that.'

'I don't want to have it. What if he turns out like Curtis?'

'He ain't gonna turn out like Curtis cos we're gonna bring him up, innit.'

When she hears me say '*we're* gonna bring him up' she smiles, reassured just a little. Lauryn hates being on her own and she hates having to do things alone.

So she starts to calm down. She says, 'You look terrible.'

'Thank you.'

'Where were you last night?'

'Chasers with Becks and her friends, innit.'

'I wish I could have a night out. But look at me. Look how fat I've got.'

Of course she ain't fat. But her belly is really big.

Before I can say anything, my phone goes.

'You're not even paying attention to me,' Lauryn says. She's getting into a proper sulk.

I'm not even looking at her. My eyes are on my phone. This is the message I've been expecting.

Sully.

'Jaq,' Lauryn shouts. 'You're not listening to me.'

'This is work,' I tell her. 'This is important.'

I have to read the message twice.

Sully wants to see me. I start typing back. Lauryn snatches my phone.

'What the fuck? That's my phone.'

'And I'm your sister. What's more important to you? Me or your phone?'

'Give me my fucking phone.'

I go to grab her hand but she pulls away from me.

'Lauryn!'

I grab her wrist and twist her hand.

'Are you going to hit me again, Jaq? Are you?'

Typical Lauryn to bring that up. That time I gave her a hiding in her bedroom at Mum's and called her a stupid bitch. But there was a reason for that as everyone knows. She almost got Sully killed cos of her loose talk. She didn't mean to, but she did and she should of known better.

'No, I ain't gonna hit you but I want my phone back.'

I get my phone off her. She bursts into tears. Proper hysterics now.

Becks comes in all sleepy. Lauryn runs to her and throws her arms around her and cries into her neck. Becks says nice comforting words and I'm texting Sully.

He texts right back.

Number One Caff in an hour.

I have a quick shower. My eyes are small and tired. My head is banging. Becks and Lauryn are on the sofa in the living room drinking tea. Becks is good with Lauryn.

I don't wanna drive the state I'm in so I call an Uber. The first one cancels and I end up getting to the meet ten minutes late.

Walking in, I'm thinking it's funny that Sully wants to meet at the caff. Cos the caff is Dushane's office really. It's where the top boy does his business and when I see him in there, where Dushane always is, it fully dawns on me, yeah it's true. Sully has taken over.

I sit down opposite. 'Wagwan.'

'You're late,' he says.

'I was having a situation with my sister.'

'You're telling me this because?'

'Because that's why I'm late.'

Sully just looks at me.

'Sorry I'm late,' I say.

'What have you heard?'

'Well,' I start. I'm thinking, is there anything I've heard that he's gonna think I shouldn't of heard? But I can't play dumb and say I ain't heard nothing cos Sully knows how word gets around. People talk, even if half that talk is total bullshit.

'I heard Jamie got laid out.'

Sully nods slowly. 'Yeah, I heard that.'

I mean, come on. I'm looking at the man who right at that moment I knew a hundred per cent was the one who switched Jamie off and we're both pretending it weren't him.

'Was bound to happen,' I say. 'Sooner or later.'

Again, he nods.

'Could have been anyone done it,' I say when he doesn't say anything.

'I need you to do something.'

'Yeah?'

'What I'm hearing is the brothers think they saw someone. They're gonna be upset. Obviously. And when people are upset they can get things wrong and say things they shouldn't say. But obviously Aaron and Stefan can't tell anyone who they think they saw, whoever they think it was. Most of all they can't tell the feds. Cos that would break the code.'

You ask any roadman about breaking the code and they'll all say the same thing, no, you can't break the code, like it's a commandment in the Bible. But if you ask them what the code is, they have no idea. No one knows what's in it or who made it up or when. But we're all supposed to live by it. This so-called code.

But I knew that Sully meant the brothers had to keep their mouths shut and if the feds asked them if they saw whoever it was that shot Jamie in the head they had to say no.

'That would break the code,' I parrot back.

'The feds have already had a quick talk to them,' Sully says. 'And they didn't say nothing, which is the correct thing for them to do. But the feds ain't gonna give up that easy. They're gonna be back. So you're gonna go and tell Aaron and Stefan to keep their mouths shut, innit.'

'Me?'

'Yeah, you.'

'Why?'

'Cos I'm telling you.'

Fuck me. Hangover. Lauryn. Now this. This is the day from hell.

'All right. Where are they? They're not still at the flat, are they?'

'Nah, that's a crime scene. They're at Mandy's.'

'What are they doing at Mandy's?'

'They ain't got no other family, innit. So Mandy's is a safe place for them.'

Mandy's? Fuck. That's complicated. Mandy was in the bin a lotta years on a manslaughter thing. And what happens just a few days before she's due to come home? Dris, her partner – Dushane's partner, in a business sense, from the old days, from the Bobby Raikes and Lee Greene days, which means he's Sully's partner . . . and friend – Dris gets shot dead on top of the high rise in Summerhouse.

Dris broke the code.

No one seen who pulled the trigger. There was no cameras. No prints. No DNA. But if I say there was a beef between Dris on the one side and Dushane and Sully on the other, you get the picture.

'Anything in particular you want me to say?' I ask Sully.

'You know what to say, bruv.'

'Cool.'

He looks at me like the meeting's over. I don't move just yet.

'What's Dushane saying about Jamie getting switched off?' I ask, keeping it casual.

'You ain't gonna be seeing a lot of Dushane from now on.'

For a split second, I'm thinking, fuck me, he's done Dushane and all.

But then he goes on, 'Dushane's got health problems. Some heart thing, innit. He's stepping back from the road.'

'Is that why you're in here now?'

Meaning the Number One Caff, the top boy's office. Sully looks around.

'I had it swept first thing this morning,' he says. 'For bugs. Cos it ain't no secret we come in here to talk cos it's nice and private. So if I was a fed and was being nosey, this is where I'd plant a couple of bugs, innit. I told Dushane to do it but he never got round to it. Anyway, now we know we can talk without anybody listening.'

No cameras, no prints, no DNA, no bugs. That's Sully. The man is careful. His criminal instincts are very sharp. That's how come he's lasted this long. Sully's nearly forty.

That's old, and for a roadman it's very old. Like seventy for straight people.

I get up to go.

'Text me when you've chatted to the brothers,' he says. 'Then you and me need to have a proper talk.'

MANDY

Mandy's probably fifteen years older than me so I don't remember a lot about her before she went inside for the manslaughter. I was just a kid, just getting started on the road. All I know are the stories. And there's plenty of them.

Mandy used to run with a gang of girls and their speciality was honeytraps. They'd go to clubs and bars to spot a fella who looked like he had money. One of the girls – sometimes two of them – would get talking to the fella and flirt with him. Before the fella knew it he was buying them drinks, thinking he was on to a good thing.

They'd take him outside to a car or an alley, somewhere quiet. Sometimes they'd bring him to someone's yard or even a hotel. And then bang! They'd fuck him up good and rob him of everything he had, including his trainers if the girls liked the look of them.

Mandy used to carry a knife back then and I heard there was a few guys she cut up. Mandy was proper hard.

I don't know when exactly she got together with Dris but I do know that by the time she was pregnant with their daughter Erin she was on a robbery charge. It was her bad luck that she appeared at Highbury Magistrates' because they never give bail at Highbury and they remanded Mandy in custody even though she was already like six or seven months gone.

When she went into labour, they took Mandy direct from jail to the hospital and chained her to the bed, innit. Dris weren't allowed to be there. Little Erin came into the world with her mum cuffed to the bed. What kind of start to life is that?

That same day that Erin was born they took Mandy and her back to the mother and baby unit in the prison. They only allow you to keep the baby for a year or maybe two, then you can't have the baby with you no more. That's how come Erin got brought up by Dris in Summerhouse cos Mandy got time for the robbery, I can't remember how long. It weren't too long. I think she got about a five, something like that.

Dris was a good dad. You'd see him walking Erin to school every morning. One morning, he'd just dropped Erin at the gates and she was in the schoolyard playing with her friends when all these armed feds jumped him and slung him up against the school fence. Little Erin was sitting on the swings watching her dad getting frisked and then bundled into a car and taken away. I don't think she had any idea what was going on. Probably thought it was a game or something.

When Mandy got out of jail, she moved into Dris's place in Summerhouse. She calmed down a lot after the baby and they was a proper family. Dris was earning money – I mean, money money – on the road with Dushane and Sully. Dris was like partner level in the mandem, so he would of been bringing home a lotta Ps. It was all good.

Except Mandy's old girlfriends, the ones who weren't in jail, were still doing their honeytraps and one night Mandy gets roped in and it all ends up very bad with the fella getting stabbed and four of the girls, including Mandy, getting charged with murder. Even though Mandy weren't there when the fella got killed, she got done under joint enterprise. The murder eventually got knocked down to manslaughter and Mandy ended up doing eight, nine years.

And then, like a week before Mandy was due to come out of prison the second time, Dris gets laid out.

Now, I ain't admitting nothing. But this is something I know a little bit about. Don't ask me no details.

Dris was OK, but he thought he was due more than he was getting. He started complaining that Dushane and Sully weren't taking him serious as a partner. They weren't giving him no respect. He even started looking at me funny, like I was responsible for his situation. But the truth is Dris weren't half the roadman he used to be. He'd had a stroke from doing too much nos. He put on weight. He was losing his hair, his eyesight was going. He was one of those men who gets old young. He slowed down. Course Dushane and Sully were looking at him differently. When you're top boy, you need reliable people around you. And Dris weren't reliable no more.

I was.

So they asked me to step up and Dris got sidelined even more. Not even the youngers respected Dris. He was kind of pathetic and sad. He was still a good dad, though. He'd still walk Erin to school and pick her up, even though when she got bigger it was embarrassing for her in front of her friends to still have her dad bringing her to school. But he loved that girl.

Then Dris did a very wrong thing. Right in the middle of the war between Summerhouse and Jamie's Fields mandem, Dris sets up Dushane and Sully to get hit in the Number One Caff. That was wrong.

Even Dris knew it was wrong. And he also knew that if Jamie missed Dushane and Sully there'd be a price to pay.

Which is exactly the way it went down.

Jamie and his soldiers ran into the caff mob-handed. But Dushane was already way ahead of them. He was sitting in a car across the street with Sully watching the whole thing. And the two of them knew right then who the traitor was.

What they say is that some mysterious figure called at Dris's door right after the thing at the Number One Caff, maybe the same mysterious figure that called at Jamie's door. If you get what I'm saying?

The very second Dris opened his door he knew.

But there was nothing he could do.

The mysterious figure told him it could go down somewhere quiet or it could be right on the doorstep where Erin would see. Erin, who would of been thirteen or fourteen then, was watching TV while this was going on at the front door. She'd hear the shots and she'd find her dad dead on the doorstep.

Is that what Dris wanted?

Nah, he didn't want that. No one wants the kid they love with all their heart to find them lying dead by the door with their head blown off.

Dris asked if he could put some shoes on. The so-called mysterious figure said no, stop wasting time.

So Dris walked with the man he knew was gonna lay him out and they went up the tower block.

I ain't relying on rumour here cos I saw this part with my own eyes. Dris wasn't shaking or crying or begging for mercy, or anything like that. He was calm. I respected him for that.

He broke the code. Even I would have to say that. He done wrong and he took his punishment. He took it on the chin.

It was one shot to the head. But when people talk they never play things down. They always play them up. They exaggerate all the time. The next morning the youngers were talking about how Dris got riddled with like twenty or thirty bullets.

Mandy came home from jail a few days later. Social services had already taken Erin into care and the council had taken the flat cos the tenancy was in Dris's name, not Mandy's.

Mandy had no man, no daughter, no house. They put her in a hostel on Jane Street, a very dodgy place, full of cons, snitches and nitties.

Mandy used to scare me, I can't lie. She had a big rep. And because of what happened to Dris, I didn't wanna cross paths with her. Mandy didn't know who switched Dris off, but it don't take a genius to work out that it had to be Sully or Dushane cos you can't lay out one of the mandem without the top boy giving the go-ahead. And Mandy knew I was rolling with mandem so she would have her own ideas about me.

Sully told me one day when he was living on that canal

boat he used to live on that he went to the hostel and put an envelope in Mandy's hand that had a lotta Ps inside.

Mandy asked him if it was blood money. She asked him to his face if he shot Dris.

Sully denied it of course. He wants her to have the money. But she gives it back to him. She told him her life weren't about that no more.

Respect for Mandy. I mean, she's living in a shitty hostel full of nitties and the money would of come in handy. It was enough for a deposit and she could of rented a nice flat and got Erin back, which is what she wanted.

But she said no.

Then I heard that Sully talked to Shelley about giving Mandy a job at the nail bar and bit by bit Mandy starts putting her life together again. She gets a flat not too far from Summerhouse and social services let Erin come and live with her. She's turning her life around. She has nothing to do with them girls and their honeytraps. She won't even see them for a drink cos with them girls one thing could easily lead to another and this Mandy is a different person from the old Mandy.

She's not even looking to find who laid out Dris. She's let that go. This makes me feel a bit calmer about going to her house like Sully told me to.

The flat's on the ground floor of a low rise not too far from the Number One Caff so I just walk round there.

AARON, STEF AND ANGELA DAVIS

With Black people, when someone dies people come round the house to show respect. The door's open or it's on the latch and people come in and out bringing food and drink. You'll see people hanging around outside, maybe smoking, maybe just chatting, telling stories.

But when I arrive there weren't no one there. Even though it's not where Jamie and his brothers lived, people would of heard that Aaron and Stef had gone to Mandy's and they'd be here to pay their respects. I'm starting to think maybe Sully got it mixed up and it weren't Mandy's that the brothers went to. Except Sully don't really ever get mixed up.

I knock on the door.

Mandy opens. Her look ain't unfriendly but it ain't exactly warm either. I can see she's surprised to see me at first. But then, I can see her putting it together. She knows I roll with Sully and Dushane so it ain't surprising I'm here.

'Wagwan, Mandy,' I say.

'Wagwan,' she says. She's only saying it to be polite. 'What are you doing here?'

'I hear the brothers are here.'

Mandy's look is hard now. I can see the old Mandy in there. The Mandy that used to carry a knife. You can see what a scary bitch she used to be.

'What do you want with them?' she says.

'Nothing. Just got a message for them, innit.'

'Tell me. I'll make sure they get it.'

'Mandy, you know I can't do that. It has to be to them.'

'Who's the message from?'

'Mandy, you're not hearing me. You know how this runs. I've got a message and the brothers have to hear it. It's for their own good. You know that.'

Mandy looks at me like I'm a piece of shit, but she also knows that she can't get in the way here cos if she does it won't be her that suffers. It'll be Aaron and Stef.

'I have to tell you I'm disappointed in you, Jaq.'

'Like I give a fuck.'

'How old are you?'

'What?'

'You must be what twenty-six, twenty-seven? I was hoping you'd of seen through all this gang bullshit by now.'

'I don't know what you're you talking about,' I say.

'Oh, we're playing that little game, are we? Where we all pretend there ain't no gangs and nobody gets stabbed up or shot.'

'Mandy, I need to talk to the brothers and I need to talk to them now.'

She looks at me a long time before she lets me in.

The brothers are in the living room. Aaron, the older brother, is the quiet one. He's just finished uni and he's never had anything to do with the road. He's a serious kid. Reads his books and stays outta trouble.

Stefan's still at school. He's more cocky and he's had some scrapes on the road already. Including with me, although this ain't something I like to think about cos of the way it ended. This kid Attica – Ats, they called him – was good friends with Stef. Ats' mum Amma worked in the hospital but she lost her job when the Immigration people started making problems for her so money was tight at home and Ats was looking to make some Ps on the road. This was right in the middle of the war with Jamie and the Fields mob so I started thinking Ats could be useful for us. Through him we could get to Stef and through Stef to Jamie. And that's how it worked out. We got to Jamie big time. We gave Ats a bag of straps and food which he left at Jamie's yard. Then the feds got tipped off. They raided the yard, found the straps and the food, and the brothers got pulled in even though they knew nothing about anything. Jamie had no choice but to turn himself in and claim the stuff was his. It was either that or Aaron and Stef would go to jail.

I won't say who tipped off the feds cos there's people out there on the road who think talking to the feds for any reason, even to take down the opps, breaks the code. I know Sully didn't like it. But you have to hand it to whoever it was made that call. It did for Jamie. The war was over.

I don't like to think about this cos of what happened later with Ats. Kid was mouthy and he started disrespecting Stef and showing off in front of him. One day, it was the exact same day Jamie got out of the pen, Ats goes missing. The builders find his body in a skip on Summerhouse. Dushane was not happy. Not because he liked the kid, but because Dushane made it known the kid was not to be touched. And somebody touched him, which is a massive disrespect.

In the end, it turned out it was Jamie's best mate Kit who got some fella to bad Ats up a little as punishment for the way he was behaving with Stef. The fella went too far and killed him and I can't help feeling bad about it cos obviously I never had nothing to do with Ats getting killed. But I was the one who brought him onto the road, innit.

I can still see Amma going round asking everyone if they've seen Ats. The woman was desperate. Her child was missing. She pulled me and I was harsh with her. I told her no, I didn't know where Ats was. Cos that was the truth. I didn't. But I ain't proud of that whole thing.

Later, I heard Stef got mixed up with this mad girl Tia who took a strap she shouldn't of taken and the two of them tried to sell it to some gangsters. Naturally, it got messy and they nearly got themselves killed. Stefan could not be more different from Aaron. He's a loose cannon. You don't know what way he's gonna go.

Stefan's eyes are all puffed from a lotta tears. Aaron don't look like he's been crying at all. They're sitting on the sofa watching TV.

'Wagwan,' I say.

Their eyes flick up at me, but they ain't interested.

'Jaq says she's got a message for you,' Mandy says.

They keep their eyes on the TV.

I hear Stefan grunt something back. I turn to Mandy and jerk my head to the kitchen. She don't move.

'Mandy, this is a private conversation between me and Aaron and Stef.'

Mandy says, 'If Aaron and Stefan want me to go, I'll go. Do you want me to go?'

The brothers shake their heads.

'I'm staying,' Mandy says.

It's a challenge to me. If I want her out, I'm going to have to escalate this and I don't want to have to tangle with Mandy, especially with how delicate I'm feeling right now. My head is still banging.

'All right,' I say. 'Don't matter.' I turn to the brothers. 'I'm sorry about Jamie, but you gotta hear this.'

They're making a point of not paying me no attention so I take the remote and turn the TV off. Now they're looking at me.

'I got a question for you,' I say. 'The feds ask you about what happened?'

'Yeah,' Aaron says quietly.

'They ask you if you saw who done it?'

'I told them I didn't see anyone,' Aaron says.

'Good. You done the right thing. What about you, Stef?'

Stefan gives a moody shrug. 'I didn't see no one, innit.'

'Good,' I say. 'Cos we're gonna find whoever done Jamie and we're gonna deal with it in-house.'

Aaron looks at me as if I'm chatting shit. Which I definitely am. But this is the script. He has his lines and I have mine. We both know they're bullshit, but we both gotta say them.

The look Stef gives me makes me think this boy could be trouble. He's young, he's only little. I mean, put him toe to toe with Sully and there's only gonna be one outcome, innit. But that ain't the way it works. If someone's looking for their revenge, they can wait for that moment when your guard is down. I can see them thoughts are already going through Stef's mind.

'When the feds come back and ask you again, which they will do, what are you gonna tell them?'

Stefan gets up and stomps out the room.

'Stef!' Mandy says and goes after him.

It's just me and Aaron.

'I told you,' he says. 'I didn't see who it was so when they come back I can't tell them anything different.'

'Cool,' I say. 'Same goes for anyone else who asks, right? Cos you know the way fake news gets around. Someone says someone else done something even though they didn't. We gotta catch that in the bud, innit.'

'I hate everything you people do, but I'm not a snitch,' he says.

'Take care,' I say.

I throw him the remote and go to the door.

Mandy comes running out calling after me.

'Who told you to come round here with that message?' she spits at me.

'Mandy, you know you can't even ask that. It's a message and they had to hear it.'

She's small, like me, only heavier. I can handle myself, but I don't want to have to fight her and she's fuming, she's looking like she wants a fight. I check to see if she's got anything in her hands, like a knife. But she ain't.

Her expression and her voice are very emotional.

'When I said I was disappointed in you, I meant it. Cos people tell me you're an intelligent girl and that you've got a thinking head.'

'I can't help what people say.'

'How do you feel doing Sully and Dushane's dirty work for them? Coming round here when those two boys have just lost their brother? You know both their parents died? They ain't got no one, they ain't got no other family, and you come round here and threaten them when they're grieving for the brother who brought them up and provided for them.'

'I didn't threaten them. I didn't make no threats.'

'Jaq, please listen to me. One day, someone's gonna come round to your sister or your mum or your girlfriend and they're gonna deliver the same message that you just gave to Aaron and Stef. They'll say, I'm sorry about Jaq, but keep your mouths shut.'

I snort a laugh to tell her how ridiculous this is.

'Jaq, the road you're on, you're gonna go to jail or you're gonna get killed. It's gonna be one or the other. Trust me. I've been there.'

'You ain't got no idea what you're talking about,' I say.

I turn to go. She grabs my arm. She's strong.

She says, 'Do you know who Angela Davis is?'

'Who? She ain't from the ends?'

'Nah, Angela Davis ain't from the ends. Do you know who George Jackson is? W.E.B. Du Bois? Frederick Douglass? Elouise Edwards? C.L.R. James?'

'What is this, *Who Wants to Be a Millionaire?*'

'Malcolm X?'

I don't know who the first ones are, but I've seen the film with Malcolm X. All I can remember about it is it had Denzel Washington in it.

'You're telling me you ain't heard of any of them people?'

'Nah.'

'What about Frank Crichlow? Darcus Howe?'

I heard Mandy got political in prison, but what the fuck has politics got to do with me? I'm starting to get annoyed.

'Bernadette Devlin? You heard of her?'

I look down at Mandy's hand gripping my arm to let

her know she has to let me go now or this is gonna escalate. She lets go.

'I suppose it makes sense,' she says. 'I hadn't heard of any of them people when I was your age. I hadn't read any of their books. I did that in jail.'

I've got no idea what she's talking about.

'I just wish I'd started reading their books and finding out about their lives when I was young. Cos if I'd heard what they have to say, I would of educated myself earlier and I would of gone a different road. What I'm saying to you, Jaq, is you're on the wrong road and any time you wanna talk, about anything, you can come to me.'

'What, like you're a life coach? You've got all the answers?'

'No, Jaq. No, I don't. That's not what I'm saying. But I've read a lot and I've learned a bit. And I don't want you to have to learn the way I did. The hard way.'

In the Uber, I text Sully to tell him the message is delivered and it's all cool.

I wanna sleep for a week.

My phone pings. It's Sharon.

Sharon the fed.

Asking if I've seen her earlier message. The bitch can see the double green tick. She knows I've read it.

Sharon the fucking fed.

She asks can we meet today?

No! I do not wanna meet this bitch.

My phone rings. It's Becks.

I jump in. 'Babes, this bitch Sharon, she keeps texting me saying she wants to talk about something and I ain't got nothing I wanna talk to her about.'

'Where are you?'

'I'm serious. I don't wanna talk to her.'

'Jaq, where are you?'

'I'm in the Uber. I'll be home in fifteen minutes.'

'Don't come to mine. We're at the Homerton.'

'What? Who's at the Homerton?'

'Lauryn's waters broke. She's in labour.'

That is just so like Lauryn. Fucking inconsiderate. She couldn't time when her waters broke, obviously, but it's typical that they broke now. When I'm feeling like death. The girl is so selfish.

I tell the driver we're going to the Homerton.

MUM, DAD AND JIMMY

On the way into the hospital, I glance to the left into A&E and I think I should maybe join the queue cos I am feeling really ill.

But instead I go up to the maternity unit. I know it well cos I always come with Lauryn on her appointments. There's this midwife Kath, she's Scottish, who's very easy on the eye and is always very friendly to me, and I'm pleased to see she's on duty today. She brings me to the room where Lauryn is laying in the bed and Becks is sitting beside her attending to her every need. There's a pile of glossy magazines on a chair.

I give Becks a kiss and then Lauryn. Lauryn is wearing full make-up and eyelashes. She does not leave the house without make-up.

'Where have you been?' Lauryn asks like it's the law I have to tell her where I am 24/7.

'At work,' I say. 'Some of us have jobs, you know.'

'I thought you were going to miss the baby being born.'

'I'm here, ain't I? Does Mum know?'

Lauryn makes a face. 'I tried calling and I texted her

like twenty times, innit. She said it ain't exactly convenient for her to get here but she'd try.'

We look at each other. That's Mum.

'Well, at least she replied for once, I suppose,' Lauryn says.

'Is this gonna be a long ting?' I ask.

I meant it to come out funny but Lauryn looks like she's gonna cry.

'I'm only kidding,' I say double-quick.

I turn to Becks. 'What are they saying about how long it's gonna be?'

'She's having really strong contractions,' Becks says.

'That's a good thing, innit?' I say.

'No, it is fucking not a good thing,' Lauryn shouts and, right on cue, she screams.

Kath the midwife comes in and has a quick look. 'Five centimetres,' she says with a big smile. 'It's all looking good.'

'How big does it have to get to?' Lauryn asks.

'Ten centimetres, then it's big enough for the baby to come out.'

'How big is that?' I ask.

Kath puts her fingers and thumbs together to make a circle.

'Oh my god,' Lauryn says and we're all looking at each other. That is very big. I don't even wanna think about it.

I know Becks is suffering like I'm suffering, from the champagne and the drugs and the late night, but Becks is always calm and positive. She's always great with Lauryn. Better than I am.

To distract Lauryn, Becks starts talking about some

famous model in one of the magazines. Then they look at photos of her online. That leads them to clothes and shoes and make-up and skin care and hair and stylists.

I sit back in the armchair and kind of zone out cos I ain't that interested in what they're talking about and anyway I'm thinking about Jamie and his brothers and about Sully and Dushane.

Trying to work out where all this is going and how it's gonna affect me.

I need to chat to Kieron soon. Work out our strategy.

My eyes are heavy. I focus on Becks. On her neck and her mouth. The way she talks to Lauryn. She is a beautiful girl, so graceful, so elegant. I know there are people who look at us when we're out together and they're looking at me and the way I carry myself and think, she's a bad bitch, how could anyone be like that 24/7?

But nothing is ever what you see at first glance. You have to look again or look deeper. Who really knows anyone? Just like there's a top boy here, there and everywhere, or someone striving to be a top boy, so there's a top girl. People look at girls like me and they think they got us pinned down, but they don't.

They don't know me or what I'm about.

Who we really are underneath the surface, what drives us, what we're really looking for, nobody can tell from just a glance. Like I say, you gotta go deeper.

I believe on our journey of life there's someone for everyone and we've just got to be lucky and ready when that person enters our lives and not be afraid to accept what we feel. Look at Sully and that boat girl, the water gypsy, the French girl Delphine. I think she would've been good for him. But he wasn't ready.

Look at Dushane and Shelley. Shell's a legit business-woman looking to stay on the right side of the road and develop not only herself but her business. The love she wanted to share with him was unconditional, but to me it never looked like he was ready.

When I met Becks I couldn't eat properly and I couldn't sleep properly cos I kept thinking about her, and when you get that feeling inside you just know. At first, I couldn't understand what I was really feeling for her, or maybe I was in denial. But I just knew deep down I had to give this a chance. It's different. More different from anything I have ever felt and, just like I do for Lauryn, I have this feeling of love and protection. Becks makes me laugh. She makes me cry. She makes me angry, but there's something very special. Me being who I am, I wouldn't admit it at first and perhaps it was because I didn't want to show any sign of weakness, but trust me it's not a weakness to show that beyond what you do you have feelings too, and I want those people who look at me and judge me to understand they don't know me. They've never really looked at me or tried to understand that I do what I have to do to survive. It don't mean I don't have humanistic feelings. It's the cards I was dealt for my journey, say no more.

Lauryn is screaming so loud I wake up thinking someone's getting murdered. Kath hurries in and does another quick check and then it goes quiet again.

You're probably thinking I'm a bad sister. I can't even stay awake for when Lauryn's having her baby. I'm happy for Lauryn but I can't lie, I wanna get home quick so I can curl up in bed with Becks. Instead, I'm in this chair and it's hurting my back. All I can hear is Becks' voice all soft and soothing, telling Lauryn it's all gonna be all right, and I fall back asleep.

I've been fighting battles since I was a very young age. I've always played the big sister role for my big sister. And soon after that the mum role too, because our mum was fighting her own demons. Seeing your mum out of her trolley more or less every other day. Knowing the company she was keeping and how it's leading her down a road that's nasty, cruel and self-destructive. But you're too young and too small to stand up and say anything. If you do, you get a slap.

It's tough seeing that. It's tough being that.

Sometimes our dad would turn up out of the blue and Mum would be all different. She'd be lighter. She'd smile. She'd cook. You'd hear her singing in the kitchen. She'd make plans. The holidays we were gonna have, the places we'd go. She'd take us out to the pictures. Take us to buy clothes. We'd be on the bus coming home and she's laughing and hugging and kissing us and telling us how proud we make her and how everything's gonna be better. And you're laughing and you can't believe you never noticed before how good the world is. That's when you start to get your hopes up. That's when you think the worst is over and you've got your mum back and she's gonna love you and protect you.

And of course what happens next is Dad disappears again and Mum presses the self-destruct button. That's when it gets totally mad. Mum takes me and Lauryn to buy clothes, but she ain't got the money and gets arrested for shoplifting and at home she's crying her eyes out, dissing Dad cos he's always partying, doing drugs, flirting with other women in front of her, how all his friends are basically gangsters. Not lowlife but top of the chain gangsters.

Like Jimmy.

Jimmy the Indian they called him, though in fact his family was from Pakistan. Or at least I think it was. I don't know how he got the name Jimmy. Jimmy did time in prison for a bank robbery. I know for a fact it was suspected that Dad was involved but Jimmy was solid and didn't give up no names. That's how come they gave him such a long sentence.

Mum was worried about money the whole time we was growing up. After the bank thing, Dad come home for a couple of days. He looked very tired and his clothes were dirty. Mum went into one about Jimmy and the robbery and said she knew Dad had money and where was it cos she needed some for us. Dad was drinking heavy. Mum did not stop screaming at him. He gave her a bad beating, broke one of her front teeth, in front of me and Lauryn.

Then he walks out not saying a word and I never saw him in the house again.

After that, everything was chaos. Mum started not coming home at night. And then she wouldn't come home in the day. She never left us no food in the house or money to buy food. The electric meter was pre-paid and that would run out too. We had no idea where she was. Sometimes I just assumed she was dead. I used to ask the neighbours for food. Pat, Dushane's mum, she would always give us something. And so would Diana, Kieron's mum, which was how I met Kieron and his mate Romy.

My back is hurting, and even though I'm asleep I'm kind of awake, at least enough to tell myself not to wake up cos I don't want to have to listen to Lauryn crying.

For some reason I'm dreaming about Jimmy the Indian. Jimmy's talking to me like he's some kind of English gentleman who went to one of them top schools. But he also dropped in real cockney slang. He had all them old words. He used to call a bank a jug. Feds were cozzers or old bill. The magistrate was the beak. Prison time was bird. He used to talk about going on the pavement, which meant robbing security vans on the pavement outside the bank. People ain't done that kind of work in a long time. Jimmy was old school. In my dream, he's all wrinkled and small. Then he starts talking to me about my dad, saying how my dad really misses me.

That's when I wake up.

For a minute, I've no idea where I am. Then I see Lauryn and Becks. Kath the midwife is at the bed with a male doctor.

Kath says, 'You're fully dilated.'

Lauryn moans and screams.

'Baby's coming,' Kath says. 'Push, Lauryn. Push.'

It looks like really hard work.

I go over to be with Lauryn. She takes hold of my wrist. I look at her nails. They're painted dark blue. Lauryn's sweating. She looks up at me with fear in her eyes. I feel so protective of her. I hold her tight. She's my sister and I love her.

All I remember of growing up was being confused and angry and not having no direction. It was just me and Lauryn.

Until Dushane come along.

DRIS AND DUSHANE

On my fourteenth birthday I got two presents. They weren't from Mum or Dad either.

Lauryn got me a top. Notice how I don't say she *bought* me a top. Cos at that time we had no money. It was one of Mum's worst times. She was very depressed and weren't coming home all that much, and when she did me and Lauryn would wait till she was asleep and then go through her bag and her pockets to see if there was any money. If we were lucky, we might find a fiver, but that didn't happen often. Usually it was just a few coins, if that.

And Dad, needless to say, he weren't around either. Fuck knows where he was.

At school I used to steal food from the other kids' lunch-boxes and share it with Lauryn till this teacher caught me, and after that me and Lauryn got free lunches so I suppose getting caught in a way was a good thing. What I'm saying is there is no way Lauryn would of had the money to buy me anything. She wrapped it up in paper I recognised from art class and she gave me a big hug.

When I opened it, though, I said, 'What the fuck's this?'

It was fucking pink.

Lauryn always dressed girlie and she wanted me to dress the same way.

'Just soften your look a bit, Jackie,' she said.

'I don't wanna fucking soften my look,' I said.

'You know people are scared of you?'

'Good,' I said.

Lauryn couldn't understand why I wanted people to be scared of me, but this brings me to the second present.

It was from Jimmy the Indian.

Jimmy would pop round the house every once in a while. At all hours. You didn't know if he was gonna turn up at two o'clock in the afternoon or four in the morning. At the time I had no idea why he used to come round. It never occurred to me that he might be sniffing after Mum cos they was both old, though they did sometimes sit very close on the sofa.

Jimmy always brought us something. Never arrive with your two arms the one length, he used to say, meaning when you come to someone's house you always have to bring a gift. He said he learned the expression from this IRA prisoner he did time with in Gartree prison.

The gift Jimmy brought me for my fourteenth birthday was a bag of weed.

He said, 'You can do what you want with it, Jaq. You can smoke it. You can share it with your friends and all smoke it together. Or, and this is my advice, you can sell it.'

I immediately liked the idea of selling it.

'How much would I get for it?' I asked.

Jimmy laughed. 'I can see that little hustler brain working away,' he said. 'We have a little entrepreneur here. I knew it.'

'How much?'

'All right,' he said. 'Do you know how to play chess?'

'What?'

'Chess. The board game.'

'Nah.'

'In chess, before you make a move you always mentally go through the options. We call them the candidate moves. Then you narrow the candidates down until you find the best one. And what do you do then?'

'You make your move?'

'Nooo,' Jimmy said. 'Even when you've found the best candidate, you keep looking for a better one.'

'A'right,' I said.

'What are your options with this bag of weed?'

'I dunno,' I said.

'Candidate number one, you sell the whole bag to one buyer. The upside is that you get a quick sale and you pocket your money. The downside is that you're not going to get as much as you could if you go for the second candidate.'

'What's the second candidate?' I asked.

'Candidate number two is you divide the weed up into small amounts and you sell them individually. Ten pound a bag. It's top quality. The disadvantage is that it'll take longer. The advantage is that you'll make more money. What do you want to do?'

I didn't even have to think. 'Make more money,' I said quickly.

'You're a little entrepreneur, aren't you? Good, good.'

Jimmy gave me a hug. He said, 'You're a great girl, Jaq. If I had a daughter, I'd want her to be exactly like you.'

You know what I liked about Jimmy? He was always

smiling. He was always happy. And he never wanted anything from anybody. He was a giver. He didn't take. He just wanted to be your friend.

'Your dad misses you, you know,' he said.

'If he misses me, why don't he come to see me?'

'Jaq, Vincent has certain problems with certain people in Summerhouse and it's dangerous for him to come around the ends. But he always talks to me about you. And Lauryn.'

He made Lauryn sound like an afterthought. Jimmy always made me feel special.

'Anyway, I have to run,' he said. 'Now, you have to be careful selling that weed. All right?'

'A'right.'

Jimmy went off singing 'Happy Birthday to you, baby!' Smiling all the way. He had a nice voice.

Jimmy's bag of weed got me started on the road.

I didn't even think about trying to sell on Summerhouse. I wasn't stupid. Summerhouse was the mandem's territory and I definitely didn't want no beef there.

I divided the weed into twenty-seven baggies and I went to another estate down near the canal. I sold twenty-three of them before I ran into my first difficult customer. He took two bags but only gave me a tenner. I explained he was light. He tried to fuck me off so I hit him and split his lip and got both my bags back. I wasn't big but I'd started at the boxing gym and I could handle myself.

I sold the rest, except one bag which I kept for myself, and when I counted up my takings I saw that I had £310. A couple of customers, I could see they really wanted what I had so I pushed the price up, innit. And another customer wanted the pink top Lauryn got me.

Here's what happened. Couple of days later, I'm in the courtyard in Summerhouse smoking my weed when the customer with the split lip comes in with a fella named Dennis who has a couple of shotters on the estate near the canal where I was pushing my baggies.

The customer points me out, and him and Dennis cross the courtyard and come over.

'What the fuck do you think you're doing pushing weed round my ends? It ain't happening,' Dennis said. 'I didn't give you permission, did I?'

'It's a free country, innit,' I said. 'I don't need your permission until I see your name up in lights so you can just fuck off.'

He pushed me in the chest and I smacked him in the mouth. The customer piled in and the two of them got me on the ground. That was when Kieron and Romy come running out to help me. I gave Dennis a couple of good kicks in the balls so when he ran off he was not running very happy.

That night, I was walking home when someone called my name. I didn't recognise the voice at first. Then I see it's Dris.

'I saw the way you handled that prick Dennis,' he said. 'No fear.'

'There weren't nothing to be afraid of.'

'It's soldiers like you man needs to have around him. Not afraid, knows what time it is. You're a real G, on the up. I can see that.'

Back then, Dris was cool. He was skinny and good-looking and had this slow way of talking that was kind of nice. And everyone knew he was one of the top boys in the mandem. He always had Ps and dressed nice.

I couldn't believe what I was hearing. I was getting proper praise out here and I was already getting this sense that everyone who goes on the road gets, which is the sense of belonging. I was kind of overwhelmed, even if that sounds dumb. But I was. It's hard to explain. I knew that whatever Dris was offering I was buying, but I wasn't gonna say, not straight off. That's not how it's done out here.

So I didn't say anything, just kind of looked a bit, Yeah? What do you want?

'Listen, I want you to do something for me. Hold this,' he said, and he put a slip of paper in my hand.

I looked at the paper. It was a telephone number.

'Call me,' he said.

'I'll think about it.'

'This is just the beginning, little man,' he said. 'Go on.'

I walked the rest of the way home thinking I could not believe what was happening to me. I knew then Dris was already on to who I was without saying it. He called me G and I loved it.

Dris put me to work, shotting with the other youngers, and for a while I was making good Ps. But then there was this problem between the mandem and some Albanian gangsters which led to some people getting shot dead and this young boy Michael getting thrown off a balcony. After that, the mandem had to buy their food off the Albanians. And after the Albanians it was the Turks. Their prices went up and the mandem's profits went down. Dris was a good soldier, but he weren't a general. There was no way he could get the mandem back to what they were. Things just kept going down. Nobody on Summerhouse was making any Ps, including me.

Things didn't change till Dushane come home from Jamaica, where he had to go and lie low after the thing with the Albanians. He'd been away a long time and he didn't even remember me. Dris had to remind him who I was, and cos he was being a prick with me, I pretended I had no idea who he was. He thought I was being disrespectful, and I was. I could be very cheeky like that. He only started taking notice after I introduced him to Lauryn and she told him about this house where the woman had a lotta jewellery and shit and how he could easily rob it.

Soon after Dushane come home, Sully was back, and then things started to change. The mandem was making Ps again. It was a whole new beginning for me. This was my opportunity to protect me and Lauryn and begin our true journey.

THE BANDO

The first night after we get home from Homerton Hospital Lauryn's baby doesn't wake up once. The second night he wakes up a couple of times but he goes back to sleep again straight off.

Lauryn says how lucky she is to have a baby that's a good sleeper. Cos Lauryn really needs her sleep. The third night is a nightmare. The baby cries so much we don't know what to do and we think maybe we should call the ambulance.

I know being a new mum is hard. But Lauryn is finding it really hard. She's exhausted and crying the whole time. She keeps staring at the baby. 'He looks like Curtis, doesn't he?' she says.

'No, he don't,' I say.

'You never see likeness anywhere,' she says.

'And what's more,' I say, 'I don't know who you're talking about.'

'I'm talking about his dad, about Curtis.'

'Lauryn, that man is gone. What happened happened. Forget about him. Man never existed.'

'How can I forget about him? Every time I look at the baby I can see him.'

Thank god for Becks is all I can say. She knows how to talk to Lauryn and get her out of them morbid thoughts.

I'm still getting texts from Sharon. Sharon the fucking fed. She says she wants to meet urgent. In the end, during a brief moment when there ain't no dramas with Lauryn, I decide to talk to Becks about it.

'I don't know this girl,' I say. 'And I don't know what she wants.'

'I don't really know her very well,' Becks says. 'She's only in our circle because she's going out with Lucia.'

'She's a fucking fed.'

'Yeah, I know. She's a detective.'

'So what does she want? She's been texting me every day for a week.'

'I don't know. But why don't I talk to Lucia, see if she knows something?'

I tell her that would be cool and then I go to work.

I've got a job to do and Sully fully expects me to do it. On the road, there ain't no maternity leave or paternity leave. You gotta be on it, don't matter what's happening at home. Like Kieron's mum Diana is basically dying of cancer. I don't know how long she's got. Kieron says when they ask, the doctors never give them a straight answer. They just say things like she's responding well to the medication, there's another drug that's just been licensed that we can look at if this one doesn't reduce the tumours and so far there's no sign it's spread into any more organs. Which basically is just bullshit and a way for them to avoid answering the question you're asking.

Kieron looks after his mum. He takes her to the hospital

for her appointments and he puts all her medication in the pill organiser so she takes the right one at the right time. But Kieron has to turn up for work. Don't matter about his mum. Nobody cares. You gotta be at work.

So first thing I do, I go to the bando to make sure everything's running smooth. We change the location every couple of weeks just in case it gets spotted by the feds or by some gangsters who fancy their chances and think about robbing it. Like Curtis and his mad sister Vee and that nutter Speaks did that time. When Dushane come and saw what happened, the Ps and all the food robbed, I thought he was gonna have a heart attack. Cos man had more bad news on top of the bando getting robbed. He got a message from his brother, or maybe it was Shelley, I can't remember, that his mum had just died. Dushane leaned over the walkway, he was proper weak, and I seriously believed he was gonna drop. Some problem with his heart, innit, although Dushane never said himself cos he didn't want people to know. On the road it's like the jungle. If the pack sees the leader is in trouble, they're gonna think about getting a new leader soon. So Dushane never admitted there was a problem.

After that time Curtis robbed the bando, Sully brought in a fella for security. Ray. Ex-Army. Looks like a nightclub bouncer. He tells all these war stories about being in Afghanistan and Syria and that. Personally, I don't believe even half of it's true. Don't matter as long as he does his job, which is to protect the bando.

Depending who's working, the bando can be kind of fun. You're cutting the food and wrapping it up and counting the money, but there's always time to kick back and have a laugh. When I get there, Kieron and Romy are already there and they always make me laugh.

Romy's a little skinny guy, but he has a big heart and I ain't never seen him walk away from a fight. It was Romy who come up with the idea of using empty cans and bottles for the food. Obviously, when you're shotting on the corners the danger is that the feds will spot you and give you a spin. That's why you can't never have no drugs, no weapons on you. But obviously customers are coming to you to get their food so you need to have your stash somewhere near.

Sometimes, the shotters will hide the wraps in the back of their throat. I knew a girl who could hide twenty wraps in her mouth that way. But the feds know that trick now and they force your mouth open to look inside and all the shotter can do is swallow it and hope the wraps don't burst. It's a big risk cos if they burst inside you, you're fucked.

Sometimes, you'll have one of the youngers on a bike and you give him the order and he goes off to collect it from one of the mandem nearby. But again, the feds are looking out for this pattern and they will sometimes stop kids on bikes and search them.

Basically, no one wants to get caught in possession. But you need to be in possession so you can do business.

So Romy came up with this idea of collecting up all the cans and bottles that was thrown away and then slipping different drugs into the different cans. Like, if it's an orangeade can we'll put a wrap of white in there. Two wraps in cola cans, five in lemonade cans. And different cans for dark and weed. Then we put the cans in a black bin bag and we leave it across the street from the corner, where we can still see it but far enough away so that when the customer comes we say, go over to the bag and take whatever it is depending on the order. And if the feds come, we just go, nah, nothing to do with us, mate.

So there's always a lotta cans and rubbish being sorted in the bando and it's so disgusting that all you can do is have a laugh while you're doing it.

Meanwhile, Ray sits in a battered old stained armchair reading the *Daily Mail* and superhero comics.

I nod to Kieron and Romy and we go into one of the bedrooms. We need to have a serious talk. The only furniture is two old plastic chairs. I sit on one and Romy on the other. Kieron stands by the door.

First thing we need to discuss is if there's gonna be any comeback from the Fields lot for Jamie.

'Nah,' Kieron says. 'They ain't gonna try nothing. Even if they wanted, they don't have the muscle, innit.'

'I heard Si's running things now,' Romy says.

'Si ain't gonna be a problem,' Kieron says. 'He don't have the balls.'

'What about Stefan?' I say.

'That little runt?' Kieron says.

'What's your problem with little runts, bruv?' Romy says, pretending to be serious cos he's a little runt. 'Little runts can be dangerous, trust me.'

'That's what I'm thinking,' I say. 'Stefan gave me a look when I went to talk to them. The older brother, Aaron, he don't wanna know. He ain't gonna be a problem. But Stefan, we need to keep an eye on him.'

'Anyone seen Dushane?' Romy asks.

I haven't and neither has Kieron.

'I mean, is man gonna accept that he ain't top boy no more?' Romy says. 'Cos, fuck me, I mean this is Dushane's business really.'

The three of us have a bit of a disagreement about which of them, Sully or Dushane, done most to build the business up. I think it was Sully, but Romy says that without Dushane the Summerhouse mandem would never have been as big as it is.

'The two of them were a team,' Kieron says. 'They did it together. It's a shame they broke up like this.'

Kieron seems genuinely sad that Sully and Dushane have split. And I see his point. Dushane and Sully, Sully and Dushane, they were a great team.

'Question is, is Dushane gonna make a move?' Romy says.

They're arguing back and forth when my phone pings. Sharon the fed wants to meet.

SHARON THE FED

Sharon and me meet in Victoria Park by the pond.

'Thanks for making the time, Jaq,' she says. 'I appreciate it.'

'Say less. What's up?'

'Look, Jaq, what I'm going to say is going to sound funny. But I'll hope you'll hear me out.'

'A'right,' I say.

I'm already suspicious.

'First, I want you to know this is not a set-up. This is not a police operation. It is just you and me talking.'

She opens her coat to show me, I suppose, that she ain't wired up.

'You can search me, you can take my phone, whatever you want.'

I look around to see who might be watching, but it's just the usual crowd: hipsters drinking coffee, yummy mummies with their kids, joggers and people with their dogs. I can't see no one paying me any special attention.

But it makes sense to be careful.

'Gimme your phone,' I tell her.

'Sure,' she says and hands it over.

It's not a smartphone. It's an old Nokia.

'This is your phone?'

'It's my phone.'

'What's the password?'

'Six one nine one.'

It unlocks.

'Go ahead, you can read the messages if you want. The only ones on there are with you and a colleague.'

'It's a burner?'

'Yeah.'

There ain't more than six or seven messages, most of them to me. I turn it off and give it back to her. I go through her pockets. Keys, coins, chapstick, crumpled paper tissues. I go through her bag. Usual crap.

'This isn't being recorded,' she says. 'Believe me, the last thing I would want is for this to be recorded because I am taking a big risk here.'

'A'right,' I say. 'What do you want?'

'This is between you and me. It doesn't go any further unless we come to an arrangement.'

'I ain't gonna tell anyone.'

I'm gonna tell Kieron, of course. Everything. But probably not Becks, depending on what it is.

'I don't know if Becks told you but I work out of Wembley.'

'She didn't say anything about that.'

'Well, one of my colleagues knows about a consignment that's coming in. It's worth a lot of money.'

Fuck me. I don't know what I was expecting but I was not expecting this.

'And I wondered if you might be interested?' she says.

Sharon is looking a little nervous. But in a good way, for me. Not nervous as in she's putting on an act and this a trap. Nervous as in she's out of her depth. It makes me think this is genuine.

'Why would I be interested?' I ask her.

'You or maybe someone you might know. I don't know. Someone in your circle. I'm not trying to be funny. It's just there's an opportunity here and my colleague and I need a little help from somebody and I thought maybe you could be that somebody.'

I don't say anything.

She continues quickly, 'If I'm barking up the wrong tree here, Jaq, I'm sorry. I don't mean to cause offence.'

I'm also a little nervous. Fuck me, I'm talking to a fed about ripping off some roadman's drugs. Who wouldn't be nervous? But I'm also curious.

'How much is the food worth?' I ask.

'We've been told it has a street value of between five and seven mil.'

Five to seven mil? Now I'm nervous, curious and very fucking interested.

'What kind of help are you looking for?'

'The consignment is arriving any day now. We know the address it's going to. Someone will have to go into that address and take the stash. They'll also have to sell it because me and my colleague, we don't have those kind of contacts, and, frankly, we don't want them.'

'How much are you and your colleague looking for?'

'We want an upfront finder's fee.'

'How much?'

'One mil.'

'Upfront?'

'Upfront.'

'I can tell you now, Sharon, one mil upfront ain't gonna run. No one has that much Ps lying around.'

'We could talk about the upfront money, as long as we have a guaranteed payment for the rest.'

'How much are you looking for?'

'Half the street value.'

I make the next bit up cos I ain't never been in a position like this before.

'That's a lot more than the going rate for a tip-off.'

'We do want to be properly compensated,' she says. 'It has to be fair. I mean, without our information no one gets anything.'

'Without someone going into the address no one gets anything,' I point out to her. 'And that someone is gonna be taking a big risk.'

'Fair enough. We're prepared to negotiate.'

'What's in the stash?'

'Charlie and horse.'

This makes me laugh. Jimmy the Indian used to call it charlie and horse. Jimmy with his old-fashioned words.

'When's it arriving?'

'We don't have a precise date yet, but it's going to be sometime in the next ten days. Could be a bit earlier, could be a bit later. That's why I've been pestering you. Sorry. But it's a golden opportunity and they don't come along that often. What do you think? Are you interested?'

'You and your friend at the station are running a risk,' I say.

'I know. But the way we look at it, the reward is worth it. And who knows? Maybe this is a relationship we could build on. This isn't the first time we've had information like this, and it won't be the last.'

'You and your friend are running a risk, which means I'm running an even bigger risk,' I say. 'Cos if this comes back to you and your friend, the first person you're gonna give up is me.'

'That's not going to happen. First off, it's not going to come back to us. We've been very careful about covering our tracks. We're using burners and payphones. Secondly, even if it did come back to us, say we got nicked, although that is not going to happen, we know how it works, how cases are made. We're not going to admit anything because the minute we do we're sending ourselves to prison. Why would we do that?'

She can see I'm not convinced.

'Jaq, there's nothing to connect us to the consignment. No one knows we know about it.'

'So how did you find out about it?'

'One of my colleague's informants told him.'

'So you're already lying to me?' I say harshly. 'You just told me no one knows, but already someone knows.'

'All right, I should have said the informant. But he really isn't going to be a problem. He's passed the information on to his handler. The consignment gets robbed by whoever robs it. He's not going to think that it's been robbed because of us, he's not going say anything to anyone. Believe me, he's terrified my colleague will send him back to jail. He knows better than to open his mouth.'

I'm thinking all this over.

'What do you think? Do you think we can do business here?'

It's very tempting. I'm already calculating the numbers

in my head. After we give the feds their cut, we're left with between two and a half and three and a half mil. Maybe even four if the value is at the high end.

I have one more question.

'Who owns the stash?'

'A fella named Dickie Simms. He's out of Kensal Rise. Do you know him?'

'Nah,' I say, 'I ain't never heard of him. White? Black?'

'White.'

'I'm assuming if Dickie's moving that much food he's got soldiers and they've got straps.'

'Straps?'

'Guns.'

'They'll almost certainly be armed, yes, but you wouldn't be going in blind. The informant knows the location, he knows the layout and he knows who's inside with the stash at any one time.'

She waits for me to say something. When I don't, she jumps in. 'This is time-sensitive, Jaq. The consignment is coming in sometime in the next ten days. It won't be at the address for more than two or three days at the most. So if you want to come in on this, I need to know.'

'I need a day to think about it.'

Sharon was obviously hoping for a quicker answer. But tempting as it is, you always gotta consider these things carefully. There's a lot riding on the outcome and you don't want that outcome to be the wrong one. Like you end up in jail. Or dead. Which in this business can easily happen.

'I'm going to need an answer by tomorrow morning,' she says.

There's a hard look about her, a kind of fed look that I don't care for. I give her a look of my own.

'This is a golden opportunity,' she says. 'For both of us. We can make a lot of money here. It's up to you.'

'I'll let you know tomorrow morning,' I say.

She holds out a phone. 'Use it to contact me from here on, whether you decide yes or no. It's pay as you go. My burner's number is already on it.'

'Sweet,' I say.

I take the phone and I walk away.

THERE'S ALWAYS A TOP BOY

When you think about it, there's always been a top boy.

Everywhere. All down through the years.

When you think about it, back in slavery times that fella on the slave ship going across from Africa to America, all chained up in the darkness with all the other slaves, the one who kept his head down and waited and watched till he figured out how it all worked and how he could get outta this.

What's the first thing he done?

He looked around at the other kidnapped Africans all chained up with him and he said to himself, nah, that one's meek, he ain't no good. That one ain't no good either, he's afraid of them white men. And that one's broken. And that one ain't got no belief. But that one, I can see the fire in his eyes and that tells me he's thinking the same I'm thinking.

So when he gets the chance, he whispers to the fella with fire in his eyes, I'm getting outta this. You coming with me? And between them they come up with another four or five men and women who have the same fire in their eyes.

And the fella talks to all of them, tells them they gotta

try. Maybe they'll win or maybe they'll lose. But losing can't be worse than what's waiting for them when they get off the ship. So they gotta try. And the fella persuades them and they make their move.

We don't know if it worked out for them or not. Maybe they killed the captain and the slavers and got control of that ship and sailed it back to Africa. Or maybe the captain and the slavers killed them and threw their bodies overboard. Who knows? But that ain't the point. The point is that the fella who waited and watched till he had it figured out and then talked the rest into it, he was the top boy.

It's about seeing the chance and then convincing other people to come with you. That's a top boy.

Or a top girl.

Back at mine, the baby is finally sleeping after a feed and me, Lauryn and Becks have dinner together. Becks has cooked up this fancy Arab Turkish food from one of her recipe books and we're drinking wine and talking and laughing. Lauryn's happy cos she's had some sleep and she's beginning to understand how this baby ting works. Everyone's happy and telling funny stories and memories, and for some reason I mention Dad's friend Jimmy the Indian and me and Lauryn tell Becks all about him.

'He always had nice clothes,' Lauryn says. 'He always smelled nice.'

'He was a character,' I say. 'I loved it when he turned up at the house. He was always so happy and you never knew what he would arrive with but he always had something.'

I tell the story of what he brought me for my fourteenth birthday. Becks can't believe it.

'You ain't got one of those little baggies left over, have you?' Lauryn says, half joking, half not joking.

'That was more than ten years ago,' I say.

'I could do with some weed now,' she says and then she gives me one of her looks. 'Jackie, please,' she says.

'No,' I say.

'Just to take the edge off.'

'No. It would be bad for the baby,' I tell her.

'But it would be good for the mum,' Lauryn says. 'I need looking after too, you know.'

Becks says she heard about this post-natal yoga class thing that's supposed to be very good for new mums. Typical of Becks that she would think of this. She's that kind of person. She thinks about other people. Specially Lauryn cos it's almost like Becks is the long-lost sister who's turned up and is sorting all the problems that have come up while she's been away.

Lauryn rolls her eyes. Which is also typical. Of her.

'Yoga's very good for stress,' Becks says.

'I'll go if you come with me, Becks.'

But the classes are at eleven and Becks needs to be at work.

'Jaq,' Becks says, 'you go with her.'

'Nah.'

'You should go,' Becks says. 'It would be good for your stress levels too.'

I say I'll think about it. I'm checking my phone. In my business, and if Sully's your boss, you gotta check your phone every five minutes. You're on 24/7. Lauryn gives me grief about it, says we're having dinner and no devices and tells me to put my phone away.

'What we gonna call the baby?' I say to get her off my back.

'I don't know,' Lauryn says. She shrugs.

And the way she says it, like she don't care what the baby's called, it's not giving me a good feeling about her and the baby.

'What?' she says, looking at me.

'I'm just saying. The baby needs a name.'

And suddenly Lauryn bursts out crying. Becks cuddles her.

'I'm a terrible mother,' Lauryn is sobbing.

Where's this coming from? I've got no idea. She just keeps sobbing about what a terrible mother she is.

'It's her hormones,' Becks says to me over Lauryn's shoulder. 'They're all over the place.'

'I'm trying so hard,' Lauryn sobs.

'I know,' I say. 'You're a great mum.'

We get her to calm down, making stupid jokes and telling her how good a mum she is and is gonna be. She sips some wine and gives this sort of brave smile.

'Do you think he looks like . . .?' She doesn't finish the sentence. I don't allow the name Curtis to be spoken in my yard.

'Lauryn, I already told you. No. Is the answer. He don't.'

'He looks so like him.'

'He don't.'

And me and Becks have to go through the whole thing again, reassuring her and comforting her. It's fucking hard work. And she's my older sister. So I tell her this story.

'Listen, I never told you this, but one time I went in Mum's bedroom and guess who was in there?'

Lauryn says all moody, 'I don't even want to think about that.'

But Lauryn loves gossip.

'Who was it?' she says, dabbing her eyes with a tissue.

'Jimmy.'

'Jimmy the Indian? Dad's mate?'

'Yup.'

'Were they actually doing it?' Lauryn asks, leaving her mouth open at the end of the question.

'I can give you the details if you want the details.'

'No!' Lauryn screams.

Then she leans in to me. 'What were they doing?'

'Come on, Jaq,' Becks says. She's on Lauryn's side. They want to know. 'What?'

'Jimmy was eating her out.'

'Nooo!'

'Yeah, he had her legs right up in the air.'

'No, no,' Lauryn screams. 'Stop it!' Finally, she's having a really good laugh.

During all of this, even when I'm telling the story, I can't stop thinking about Dickie Simms and his stash and what I should do about it. It's like Sharon said, this is a golden opportunity. It's like when Jimmy gave me the bag of weed.

Do I grab it or do I let it go?

Back in the day, way before I got involved on the road, Dushane and Sully were just two soldiers in Summerhouse. Back then, all the food sold in Summerhouse came from a white gangster called Bobby Raikes. I never knew him. But the way I heard the story it was like this.

Bobby Raikes supplied the food, but of course it goes without saying he weren't on the corners selling it himself. He left that to his guy Lee Greene. Lee started out on the road an ordinary soldier, pushing his wraps of white and dark and bringing the money back to Bobby. But soon Lee recruited some youngers and they started shotting and bringing him the money which he then brought back to Bobby after taking any profits. Two of the youngers Lee found were these two schoolfriends called Dushane Hill and Gerard Sullivan, or Sully as he is known, both from Summerhouse.

Dushane and Sully were top shotters. They sold a lotta food. They made a lotta P for Lee, which meant that they made a lotta P for Bobby Raikes.

Lee was kind of fat and lazy. Dushane and Sully were lean and ambitious. They knew they could make a lot more money outta Summerhouse if only Bobby would let them run tings instead of Lee.

Now, obviously, that didn't sit right with Lee Greene, but Bobby wanted to know who these young kids were and if they could make Ps for him. In them days, the roadmen didn't call it P like we do. That's how long ago it was. They called it paper, which if you said that now, paper, people would know you ain't from the road. Bobby was open to these two youngers stepping up. But what he wanted to know was could he trust them?

So he gave them something to do.

Bobby's nephew – or it might of been his niece, whatever, someone in his family – had got their eye poked out in a fight. The eye got poked out with a finger. Bobby told Dushane and Sully he didn't want the fella dead, he just wanted the finger and it had to be the right finger, the one that poked the eye out.

The way I heard it, Dushane and Sully grabbed the fella coming outta the barber's one night and cut off his finger. Except when they had the finger they realised it was the wrong one. So they cut off the right one and brought it back to Bobby.

After that, Bobby started to take them a bit more serious and gave them more food to sell, which they did, and they started making more and more money for Bobby. Which, naturally, made him very happy.

I don't know the full story of how it happened, but from what I heard later Dushane and Sully laid out Lee Greene. Now they were running tings in Summerhouse.

But they were still working for Bobby Raikes and that wasn't part of their long-term plan, especially when Bobby decided he didn't want to work with Sully no more.

So, the rumour goes, Dushane switched off Bobby Raikes.

I don't know if that last part's true, but what is true is that Bobby Raikes just suddenly disappeared. No one ever saw him again.

And Dushane was top boy in Summerhouse.

All cos he waited and watched until he'd figured out how things work. And then he made his move.

So the thing is, do I make my move or not?

I text Kieron. You home?

KIERON

I go Kieron's.

Diana opens up. She's wearing a headscarf cos of the chemo, but she looks pretty good actually. She gives me a big smile. Diana's always liked me.

'I hear Lauryn's had the baby,' she says.

She's so pleased it's almost like it's her own daughter who's had the baby. Diana used to bring us food back in the times when Mum wasn't around. I mean the eating kind of food. Stewed vegetable with ackee was her speciality, but also chicken and dumplings, curry goat with rice and peas, or just patties. She'd send Kieron over with the food or sometimes she'd bring it herself. She'd come in and show us how to clean up properly and she'd chat, specially with Lauryn. They were on the same wavelength about a lotta things. Clothes and fashion and that. And she didn't have a daughter of her own so that probably had something to do with it.

'Yeah,' I say. 'Beautiful baby boy.'

'I'm so happy for her. She must be over the moon.'

'Yeah, she's loving being a mum.'

I don't know why I'm saying this shit. Sometimes, with some people, they're so upfront and genuine and innocent, you say things you know they wanna hear just so you don't disappoint them.

'Are you looking for Kieron?'

'Yeah,' I say. 'Is he home?'

'Come in,' she says.

Behind her, Kieron's already coming to the door and waving me in. I give him a look to say no, we need to talk outside. So Diana goes back in and Kieron steps out to the walkway with me.

We lean on the wall looking down into the courtyard. It's getting dark. A year ago, there would of been lights on in every unit. But since the whole redevelopment thing start probably half the units are empty and boarded up with these orange metal grilles over the doors and windows to stop squatters getting in. Summerhouse looks sad these days. Run-down and kind of empty. It won't be long before the bulldozers come in and everyone's out.

I see Ralph crossing the courtyard and heading for the stairs. The lifts ain't worked in a long time and the landlords ain't in a hurry to fix them cos everything's getting flattened one day soon.

Ralph's this old white guy with a red face and grey hair. Any time I see him I try to avoid him. It ain't that I don't like him. In fact, I do. And it ain't got nothing to do with the fact that he's gay, obviously. It's just you can't get away from him, he's so hyped about the redevelopment and how corrupt the local council is and how the developers want to get rid of ordinary working-class people so they can fill whatever replaces Summerhouse with rich people who can pay them more money. Ethnic cleansing, Ralph calls it.

When there was a meeting at the community hall about the redevelopment, Ralph gave the councillors and landlords an earful. Called them out on all their lies, innit. He got the community on their feet cheering and shouting. He was proper worked up. He even set fire to the letter the landlords had sent everyone on Summerhouse telling them they had to leave. Threatening letters, Ralph calls them.

I like Ralph, but you can't have a short conversation with him. It's gonna be long and right now I don't have the time. So when he gets to the top of the stairs and onto the walkway I pretend I don't see him. He goes to his door, probably thinking I'm a rude bitch.

'Bruv,' I say to Kieron, 'someone's made me a proposition and I'm tempted but I don't know what to do.'

I tell him about the meeting with Sharon.

'Do you know who this Dickie Simms person is?' I ask.

'Nah, I ain't heard of him.'

'What that tells me is man ain't all that,' I say. 'Cos if he was, we'd of heard of him. Which means he probably ain't got a lotta army. Look, here's what I'm thinking our candidate moves are.'

I never forgot what Jimmy the Indian told me about what you do before you make a chess move. You go through the candidates, the options.

'Candidate one,' I say, 'we go through the proper channels and tell Sully.'

'That would be the correct option,' Kieron says.

'We'd rob the stash with Sully, pay Sharon off, and Sully gives us a few quid and keeps the rest for himself.'

'Yeah, that's how it would go down.'

'Candidate two is we don't tell Sully and you and me do it freelance.'

Kieron breathes out very hard and long.

'That way, after we pay off Sharon you and me split what's left fifty/fifty.'

'If Sully found out, he would not be happy with us.'

'So we make sure man don't find out. Then there's candidate three.'

'What's that?'

'Candidate three is we rob the stash and we keep everything for ourselves, somewhere between two and a half and three and a half mil each.'

Kieron likes the sound of the numbers, but candidate three is dangerous.

He says, 'You want to rip off this Dickie Simms fella and rip off a fed?'

'I'm saying it's an option we should think about.'

'Sharon's a fed, Jaq. You can't just rip off a fed and there be no comeback.'

'She's dirty, though, innit. She can't go to her boss and tell them what happened cos then she's going to jail.'

'We'd be making a lotta enemies. Sully, Dickie and Sharon.'

'So what do you wanna do?' I ask.

'Where's this Dickie Simms keeping his stash?'

'Somewhere over Kilburn, innit. Sharon didn't give the address.'

'We'd have to go in there and take it from them?'

'Well, they ain't exactly gonna come and give it to us, innit.'

'How many man's gonna be in there?'

'Sharon says when time comes we'll know what we're dealing with.'

I can see Kieron's struggling with this.

Down in the courtyard I see Mandy cutting through the estate. On her way home from the nail bar, I'm thinking.

I say to Kieron, 'Do you know who Angela Davis is?'

'Angela Davis, the American Angela Davis?'

'I don't know if she's American. Who is she?'

'She's like very political. Black Power shit. Why?'

'Nothing. Just Mandy went off on one, innit. When I went round hers to give Aaron and Stef the talk, Mandy's like, do you know who this one is? Do you know who that one is? The only name I can remember is Angela Davis. Why's Mandy spouting this shit?'

'All that time she done in the bin? Obviously, she's gonna think deep about things. Then just before she gets out Dris gets shot dead? She's looking for answers, innit.'

'She looking for answers? That ain't gonna go down well with certain people we know.'

I'm thinking of Sully, and Kieron knows that.

'The bitch needs to keep her nose outta shit that don't concern her,' I say.

'Nah, bruv. She ain't looking for answers like who shot Dris. She's looking for deep answers.'

'Like what?'

'Like . . .' Kieron kind of shrugs. 'Like why is it like this? Like why are the ends the way they are? Gangs and drugs and shit. Ain't you ever thought about that?'

'About what?'

'Like how come we're doing the shit we're doing?'

'I don't know about you, bruv, but I'm doing it so I can get ahead. And that's why I'm bringing you this Dickie Simms ting. This could change our lives, bruv. The Ps we would make off of this, we could leave the road behind.'

Kieron thinks about it.

'It's a risk,' he says.

'Yeah, it's a risk. But, bruv, we take risks every day and this is low risk for a big reward.'

Without meaning to, I'm talking myself into wanting to do this.

'You wanna do it?' Kieron says.

'Kieron, man, this opportunity has come up. And I have to ask myself am I the kind of person who's gonna play it safe and let it go by? Or am I the kind of person who is gonna go fuck it and go after it? Cos there's a big difference in them two people.'

'So which of them two people are you?' he asks.

'I need to know if you're gonna do this with me?' I say.

Kieron's always been one of them guys who takes time to think things through. He's quiet. He don't stunt. He won't say yes or no to something straight off. He likes to think about it.

'You wanna do it?' he says.

'Yeah,' I say. 'I wanna do it.'

'A'right. But let's do it without making more enemies than we have to,' he says.

'A'right,' I say. 'Candidate two. You and me do it freelance and we split it with Sharon and her friend.'

'Sounds good. We still make a lotta P.'

'You sure?'

'I'm sure.'

Kieron might take his time, but once he's made up his mind you know he ain't gonna back out.

'I'll tell Sharon,' I say.

'What about Romy? Are we gonna need him?' he asks.

'I think you and me can handle this ourselves. But you need to be ready to move quick, day or night,' I say.

'I'll be ready,' he says.

'Cool.'

I give him a hug. He's my guy. He crosses back to his door.

'Your mum's looking good,' I say, smiling. 'Whatever they're giving her in that hospital, it's working.'

'It better work,' he says. 'The doctors are saying this is the last drug she can have. They tried all the other ones and they didn't work. So if this one don't work—'

'Nah, don't even go there, blood. Anyone who looks as good as she does is gonna be with us a long time. It's gonna work.'

Kieron smiles a big smile and disappears inside.

On the way home I text Sharon that it's a yes and all she needs to do is tell me where and when.

This is gonna change my life.

THE CALL

You know sometimes the way you can put your finger on exactly when it all started to go wrong? The exact moment? Well, this is where it all goes to shit. And I mean it really goes to shit.

It starts when I get the call from Sully that morning. It's early. I'm still in bed and Becks is having another one of her marathon sleeps.

'Meet me at the shop,' Sully says.

'Now?'

'Nah, later. I'll let you know when. Those new trainers are coming in and we need to make sure they are what we were promised they would be.'

'Cool,' I say.

'Look out for my call,' Sully says and hangs up.

Of course there ain't no shop. The shop is what we call our warehouse near Canary Wharf. And it ain't trainers that's coming in. It's food. The latest shipment from the Moroccan link that Sully and Dushane set up when they was over there in Spain and Morocco last year.

It's a big load. A lotta P.

And it's coming just at the right time cos although we ain't dry we need to restock. People like to get high. Maybe with all the problems there is now in society and the economy fucked the way it is, people need to get high more often. Just to forget. Have a little fun. Have a party in their head.

But whatever the reason, there's a lotta demand out there. You'd be surprised. And we ain't talking just nitties, although there's plenty of them, trust me. We're talking just ordinary people. Young, old. Black, white. Men, women. Rich, poor. British, foreigners. We're a service industry and we need to have in stock what the customer is looking for. If we don't have it, they'll go to someone who does.

Which means you always gotta have the food to sell them. And right at that time, we was running low.

After the call, I get up and go and look in on Lauryn and the baby. Lauryn didn't get much sleep. She's down, and even though the baby is crying, Lauryn ain't doing nothing like a mum should so I pick him up and walk him round the room.

'Who's a beautiful boy, eh? You're so beautiful,' I tell him. 'You're so beautiful.'

'Is he beautiful?' Lauryn asks.

'Yeah, course he is.'

'I mean, don't you think he looks like . . .?'

'No, he doesn't,' I cut her. 'It never happened. It's over. He takes after you and he's perfect. Look at him.'

Becks comes in.

'Hi, babe,' Lauryn says.

'I think somebody's hungry,' I say.

'He's always hungry,' Lauryn says, pissed off.

'Yeah, well, why don't you try feeding him on the boob, innit,' I say.

'No,' Lauryn says. 'Not today.'

'Everyone likes boobies,' Becks says. 'I know I do.'

Becks prepares a bottle and I give it to the baby. Lauryn looks on and tries to look happy families but she's struggling. The whole thing with the baby has thrown her sideways. Becks goes to make breakfast.

'You know, I don't blame Mum for being such a bad mum to us,' Lauryn says when Becks is out of the room. 'Cos it's fucking hard, Jaq. It's really hard.' She starts crying. 'I'm a terrible mother. I don't even love my baby.'

'Course you do,' I say. 'You're just tired.'

'I don't,' she sobs. 'I don't even like to look at him. I hate when he's hungry and I have to feed him. I don't love him, Jaq.'

She's crying her eyes out, and I'm thinking I gotta go check the youngers are out there shotting the way they're supposed to and then get down to the shop to meet Sully. This is a big shipment. White, brown, weed. It's a lotta money and it's the first load that's come in since Sully became top boy. I can't be late for this.

I'm starting to get a little panicky. I leave the baby. Lauryn is still crying.

'Lauryn, listen. I gotta go now.'

She grabs my hand and holds it tight.

'No,' she says. 'Stay with me, please. Don't go, Jackie.'

I'm really starting to panic now. My sister needs me and my boss needs me. And neither of them is in the mood for excuses.

Then what happens? Sharon sends me a text: need 2 talk.

It never rains.

I try saying some soothing shit to Lauryn, but she just rolls over with her back to me and says how I don't understand.

'You don't know what it's like,' she says. 'I didn't want to be pregnant. I wanted to get rid of it. But Curtis wanted it. He wanted a son, and now he's got one he ain't here no more. It's all Curtis's fault.'

I up my tone with her. 'Lauryn, I told you never to say that man's name. He don't exist. He was a bad dream and now he's gone and he ain't coming back.'

Sometimes you just have to harden your heart. When you're in a situation you can't change, you just have to get on with it, innit.

Lauryn looks at me funny. 'Yeah, and we know who made sure he ain't coming back, don't we? Me.'

'I told you never to talk about that.'

'That doesn't stop me thinking about what happened, does it?' she says.

'Well, you shouldn't think about it, should you?'

She laughs all bitter like.

'Yeah, that's a big help. Don't talk about it, don't think about it. That's your solution for everything, innit.'

'I just mean it ain't gonna do you no good to keep thinking about it.'

'Jaq, I can't stop thinking about it. Can you not understand that?'

'Lauryn, what you have to remember is it's over. That time is gone. You're with me now, me and Becks. And the baby. You're moving on and leaving all that behind.'

'I killed him,' she says suddenly, just spitting it out before I could stop her. 'How am I supposed to leave that behind?'

I look over at the door in case Becks can hear. She don't know what went down between Lauryn and Curtis, and I don't want her to find out. I keep all that shit from her.

'I can't,' Lauryn cries. 'I can't. I think about it all the time. I have nightmares about it. I can see him with the blood everywhere.'

I wanna tell her to move on, just move on, but she's crying even more now. But still, she knows you can't say these things out loud.

Sharon texts again. I ain't got time to read it.

I say to Lauryn, 'Look at me. Look. In my eyes. Stop crying and listen to me.'

She blinks all kind of pathetic and wipes the back of her hand across her snotty nose. I hand her a tissue. I'm like her mum instead of her little sister.

'Never say nothing about what happened with him.' I never say the bastard's name to her. 'Do you understand me? Cos it can't ever get out what happened. You would be in a lotta trouble you don't ever need to be in. But it's not just you. There's other people who could get in a lotta trouble also, including me. And they would put the blame on you. So I'm telling you, you can't fuck about with this, Lauryn. It never happened.'

She's still looking up at me like I'm her mum or an auntie or a teacher or whatever the fuck.

'Tell me you understand.'

She nods.

'I need to hear you say it.'

'I understand.'

'And you ain't ever gonna mention that man again or what happened. Right?'

'Right.' She nods, trying to be brave now.

'Good.'

Then she says, 'Jaq? What if, you know, his sister, that bitch Vee, what if she comes after me? Her and that scary fucker Speaks?'

'That ain't gonna happen,' I say.

'How do you know it won't?'

'Cos man gave Vee and Speaks a very clear message, innit. They were given a choice. They could go back home and forget about it and nothing would happen. Case closed. Or, if they wanted, they could come back for round two and end up the same way Curtis did.'

I don't use his name, but I use it this time to make sure Lauryn understands that she didn't have anything to worry about.

'It's over, babes,' I say. 'OK?'

Even though she nods, I know this is serious. Lauryn can be very moody. I've seen all her moods. Crying, throwing things, screaming, shouting. But I ain't never seen her like this before.

'You know what? I'm gonna take a day off work.'

'Today?'

'I can't today. But maybe tomorrow if I can and you and me will have a day out. Sisters' day out.'

Lauryn suddenly smiles her big, beautiful smile. 'Promise?'

'Definitely.'

'What are we gonna do?'

'Sister shit.'

'We could get a little high. Maybe you know someone who could get us something? Got any contacts?' she says with a laugh.

'Don't even joke about that,' I say. 'I told you it's bad for the baby.'

She makes a face. 'It would really be nice for me. It would help me.'

'No, it would not. We're gonna do sister shit, you and me. That's what you need.'

I check the time on my phone. 'I really gotta go.'

I kiss her and check the baby again. He's well asleep.

'Get back to sleep,' I say. 'See ya.'

Becks is in the kitchen.

'How is she?' she asks.

'Tired, emotional. She's going back to sleep.'

'I heard her talking about Curtis.'

My blood runs cold when she says this. How much did she hear? Becks is straight. Not a hundred per cent straight. It ain't that she'd go running straight to the feds if she knew, but she would have a problem with it and it would complicate things between me and her.

'Nah, she didn't say anything about him,' I say. 'She's just tired.'

Becks doesn't believe me. But I don't have time to talk this through so I give her a quick kiss, grab my car keys and run.

Before I start the engine I read Sharon's messages. She's saying Dickie Simms' stash is coming in very soon. Shit. I was hoping for a bit more of a window. It's tight but it should be OK, still. Getting this shipment from the Moroccans into the warehouse ain't gonna take more than an hour. I call Kieron. When he answers, it sounds like he's just woken up.

'You awake, bruv?' I say.

He yawns and says, 'Yeah, bruv. We had a late night, innit.'

‘That thing we was talking about? It’s arriving very soon is what I’m hearing,’ I say.

‘Cool,’ he says.

‘We’re gonna need a car and all the usual shit.’

By which I mean we’re gonna need ballies, gloves and a couple of straps. Kieron don’t need it spelled out.

‘I’m on it,’ he says, yawning.

‘Don’t go back to sleep,’ I tell him.

‘I won’t.’

‘We need to be ready.’

‘I’ll get everything sorted.’

‘Laters,’ I say and hang up.

I start the car and head for the market to check on the youngers.

When I think back on everything that happened next, that call from Sully was the start of it all.

After that call, everything went totally to shit.

THE IRISH

After Sully moved up to top boy, he told me from now on I was in charge of the youngers. I'm like their line manager, innit. I tell them what spot to go to. I make sure they have the food to sell. I make sure they're protected. I make sure that they know what to do if they get stopped by the feds. Or if another gang tries to rob them. And if they have problems, they come to me.

The most important thing is they have to come back with the correct money. Always. That's the words I will always remember from when I first went on the road.

'You gotta bring me the correct money, every time,' Dris told me, all slow and serious, after I called the number on the bit of paper he gave me. I can still see him and me sitting on the low wall in the Summerhouse courtyard. It was night and cold, but I wasn't shivering from the cold. I was excited and I was trembling cos I was on the verge of something amazing.

'You come back with the wrong money,' he said in his quiet voice, 'it's gonna get political. Even if it's five pound, you gotta explain that. Five pound is not a lotta money.

But that five pound, that don't just represent money. That five pound represents respect. It represents honour. It represents trust.'

And that's the talk I give all the youth who want to shot our food. More or less every word that Dris said to me when I first started shotting. Any youth comes to me and tells me he wants to sell, I say if you fuck the money up, you will get fucked up. It ain't that complicated and you'd think it would be easy for people to understand. But you'd be surprised how many shotters come back short of money and full of excuses I ain't interested in hearing. I make sure I get the money and then I get rid of them quick. They obviously ain't cut out for life on the road.

Bradders and Samsi know about bringing back the correct money. They are top shotters. They sell a lotta food. They're a team. They go round on their electric scooters and I don't know how they do it, but they can sell whatever you give them and then come back for more.

So when I see them in the market, I tell them to get over to the square near the supermarket, same spot as yesterday. Bradders makes a face.

'Problem?' I ask.

'Bag of nitties over there,' Bradders says.

This is what happens when people think they're stars. The ego starts to get massive and they start talking back.

'Yeah, bag of nitties equals Ps, which is why we're all here, blood. So go fucking get on with it. Go on.'

They go off on their scooters. Fucking cheeky.

Sully calls.

'I'm heading to you now. Say less, say less,' I tell him.

I tell Romy to keep an eye on the youngers and I'm just leaving to go to my car when this nittie Marianne comes up pushing a baby in a pram. She looks a mess like she always does. The baby is crying and is even dirtier than her.

'Are you even washing your baby?' I say.

'Course.'

'Well, obviously not, cos it looks filthy, though.'

'I've given him the money,' Marianne says, meaning she's paid for her drugs, like that's the most important thing here. I suppose for a nittie like her it is. All she's interested in is her fix. One of the youngers slips her some brown and she turns and wheels the pram and baby away. I can still hear the baby crying when I get to my car.

It was me and Kieron who found the warehouse a year ago. Dushane wanted somewhere out of the ends that weren't connected with us where we could hold the big Moroccan shipments before the food was split up and moved to the various bandos we have dotted around the ends where it gets cut and packaged up in wraps and – our invention – old cans. It's in an area where there's a lotta warehouses and storage units. Lotta lorries coming and going and no one bats an eye. Perfect for us. Also our warehouse is set back from the road a bit, which is even better. We aren't overlooked. And all the times I've been there, I ain't never once seen a fed.

I drive through the Rotherhithe tunnel and up to the roundabout, going left and then left again into a side road. I pull in off the road and drive up to the warehouse. There's a white lorry outside. It's the same one that's delivered before, but this time there ain't no driver in the cab. Straight off this don't look right to me.

Sully pulls in off the service road and comes up alongside me. He lowers the window on the driver's side.

'Fuck knows what's going on, bro,' I tell him. 'Literally no one's here.'

We take a good look at the lorry. It just don't feel right. Sully snaps on a pair of gloves and takes a pistol from this little secret compartment he had specially made for his car. He cocks the pistol and pulls his hoodie up. I put on the gloves I always keep in the car.

Sully and me are both thinking the same thing.

One, this could be an ambush. A rival gang might of found our warehouse and be planning on robbing us. Or maybe they've robbed the lorry already.

Two, it could be a ready eye. The feds could of found the warehouse or been following the lorry from Spain and they're waiting to see who turns up to collect.

Neither option is good. But if you give me a choice, I'd take the rival gang scenario. Cos with them you've got an even chance. They might kill you, but you might kill them. If it's the feds, you might not get killed, but you don't stand a chance. Then it's jail for a very long time.

This is just to say that this is what's in our heads as we get out of our cars and go up to the lorry. We're being very cagey. We're looking around very careful, looking for that rival gang, looking for the feds.

Sully goes round one side of the lorry and I go round the other. We look in the cab but there's no one in there. The doors aren't locked. They should be but they're not.

We get to the back of the lorry. Same thing. Not locked. This ain't a good sign.

Sully keeps me covered with the pistol in case there's a nasty surprise waiting inside while I open up. We peer in. It's empty, but that's how it should be. There's a hidden compartment where they hide the food.

Sully gives me the nod and I climb inside. There's a rank smell. It ain't that strong but it ain't nice either. I use the torch on my phone so I can see what I'm doing when I take the false partition off.

There is definitely something very wrong.

'Bruv,' I say to Sully, 'there's only two boxes.'

He nods for me to open them up. I pull the first one out and drag it to the middle.

'Open it up,' Sully says.

I already know our food is gone, but I ain't sure what to expect. I cut the lid off and jerk back.

There's a fucking human head.

A fella with black hair and a beard. There's blood in his ear. I'm gagging. I think I'm gonna throw up. Sully climbs up and looks at the head.

'Fuck me,' he says.

He drags out the second box. I already know what's gonna be in there and sure enough it's another head.

'Who the fuck are these man?' I say.

'Chaash and Mounir,' Sully says. 'Moroccan links.'

I shine my torch in the second box, the one Sully opened, and see something sticking outta the mouth. A phone. And it's obvious we're meant to find it. Sully takes it out, wipes it clean and turns it on.

A message comes up: Call me. There's a number.

We jump out of the lorry. I close the back up and go to Sully's car. He's sitting behind the wheel staring at the phone.

'You gonna call them?' I ask him.

I can see he don't want to, but I can also see he's thinking he ain't got much choice. He calls the number. The ring-tone tells me whoever he's calling is in a foreign country.

'Good morning. I'm assuming this is Sully?'

The voice on the other end is calm. One of them soft Irish voices. Sully looks at me like who the fuck is this?

'How about you tell me who you are and what the fuck you think you're doing?' Sully says.

'Sully. Am I right? I heard you took over. Very popular move with the troops is what I hear.'

This fucking freaks me out. How does this Irish fella know so much? Who the fuck is this?

Sully doesn't say anything.

The Irish fella goes on, 'I appreciate the call, Sully, and I just want to make it a hundred per cent crystal clear, just so there's no chance of any misunderstanding, all right, the absolute last thing I want is to start any trouble.'

'Bruv, are you having a laugh?' Sully says. 'My grub's gone and there's two fucking heads in boxes. How can there not be trouble?'

'What I'm saying is I have a proposal. And I think when you hear it you're going to like it.'

'Nah, I ain't,' Sully says. 'I can tell you that straight. Because when someone sends man boxes with heads, instead of bricks, that ain't a proposal. That's instant war mode, my guy.'

'Listen, Sully, keep this phone. Jonny's my nephew in London. He'll be in touch with a time and place so we can sort out the details. This doesn't have to escalate. Thanks for the call. I'm looking forward to working with you. Have a great day.'

The Irish fella hangs up.

I look at Sully. 'What was that and who the fuck's he?'

Sully doesn't say anything. He's still trying to work out what the fuck has just gone down and what to do about it.

'You think we should tell Dushane?' Sully gives me a look that could kill. 'Just saying,' I add quickly.

'We're gonna take care of this in-house,' he says.

I shut my mouth, but I'm thinking it's at times like this when Dushane's thinking head comes in useful.

'Go get a crew down here double-quick to clean up this mess,' Sully says and I get out of the car.

I check my phone as Sully drives off. Missed calls from Becks, Lauryn, Romy and Kieron. What the fuck is this? There's messages as well, including one from Sharon who says we have to meet this afternoon urgent. I don't know where to start with all this.

Sometimes being everyone's line manager ain't no fucking fun at all.

I jump in the car and head back to Summerhouse.

IMMIGRATION

I'm driving back through the Rotherhithe tunnel on my way to Summerhouse and thinking about the heads of the Moroccan links in the boxes and the stolen food and who the fuck these Irish are, and it comes to me the real reason why Sully don't want Dushane involved in sorting this shit out. This is Sully's first real test as top boy and he wants to show that he can deal with it. He knew it was coming sooner or later. Because this is what gangs do. We rob from each other all the time. It's just what we do. They rob from us, we rob from them. And people get killed.

Way back in the old days when Dushane and Sully were just starting out, the Fields mandem was run by a gangster called Kamale. This is way before Jamie came on the scene. Kamale and his dogs robbed Dushane and Sully.

I wasn't around in them days but I heard things later. I don't know exactly how it happened, but the problem got settled. What I mean is Kamale disappeared, innit.

Couple of years after he went missing, the feds dug up a body out in the marshes or somewhere like that, and of course it was Kamale. Dushane and Dris got pulled in about it, but there weren't no evidence so they walked.

Likewise, a bit later there was a problem with this Albanian mob from round Green Lanes somewhere. Again, I don't know the exact details but put it this way: like Kamale, the Albanians ain't around no more. And Dushane and Sully, they are definitely still around. And that ain't even mentioning the whole issue with Jamie and his whole Zero Tolerance thing.

What I'm saying is if you're on the road you gotta accept that greedy people are gonna come looking to take what you've got. And because there's a lotta P involved, they're gonna come with an army so you gotta have an army ready to fight back.

So Sully's thinking, OK, these Irish are trying to make a move on me so I've gotta show them who's boss and I also gotta show my people that I'm the boss. Cos if the soldiers lose confidence in the top boy, then it's all over.

The only trouble is these man seem to know a lot about Sully and he ain't got no idea who they are. And he don't wanna use Dushane cos he wants to make a point. He's got a war on his hands and he wants to win without Dushane's help.

I don't know who these Irish are but I know my man Sully. And my money's on him to win, even with the odds all against him.

I'm also thinking maybe this thing with the heads is a sign.

Cos what if Sully don't win this war? Everybody loses sometime. Law of averages. And if Sully goes down and these Irish – that smooth, calm voice is in my head – end up running tings on Summerhouse, I could be out of a job, innit. Or worse. I could be dead. So it makes sense for me and Kieron to do this ting with Sharon and rob Dickie Simms' stash. If it all goes the way it should, I'd have enough to get off the road and Kieron would have the money to buy his mum the best treatment going and she would get cured of cancer.

When I imagine things like what I really dream of, I close my eyes and see the pictures in my head. If I can really see it, like it's on a big TV in front of me, then I know it's what I really want. So I come to a red light and I stop and close my eyes and I wait for the pictures to come into my head.

I see me and Becks in a nice cottage by the sea. Just the two of us. Maybe with a baby. Becks has been talking about finding a donor. I know she's thinking about a baby. I'm down with that. I can see it. Her and me with a baby. That makes me think about Lauryn and her baby and maybe she's living with us. Except living with Lauryn would drive me nuts. I love my sister, but I also need time away from her sometimes. But, yeah, me and Becks and a baby in a cottage by the sea, I like the idea of that. And a dog. Maybe even two dogs.

I'm not gonna say anything to Becks till I've got the Ps in my hand. But when I've got them, when I know I'm sitting on all that money, then I'm gonna paint the picture for her and see how she likes it. If it's what I really want, why wouldn't it be what Becks really wants too?

The driver behind me honks his horn. I give him the finger in the mirror and drive on.

I park on the road outside the entrance to Summerhouse and text Kieron: I here.

Then I'm like where is everyone? I was born and bred

in Summerhouse and I know how it works. I know its little rhythms like I know my own body's. And something ain't right. There's a kind of atmosphere, innit. Something's happening but I don't know what. I check my phone. Kieron ain't answered my text. I try calling him but he don't pick up. That's odd. Kieron always answers when I call.

I get outta the car and walk into the courtyard and the first thing I see is up on Kieron's walkway there's a crowd of people. What the fuck is this?

That's when I see the police vans around the courtyard and the feds on the walkway.

I'm fearing the worst, that Kieron's been nicked, innit. Kieron knows the drill. He doesn't keep straps or food in his house. But then I remember that I told him to get a couple of straps for the Dickie Simms ting. What if he had them in the house when the feds came? I call him again but he doesn't pick up. Which makes me extra nervous.

Then I see Romy in the courtyard.

'Wagwan. What the fuck's going on, blood?' I say.

Romy shows me a video on his phone. I can't believe what I'm seeing.

'Immigration and feds are at my man's yard,' Romy continues. 'They're trying to take man from his home for no fucking reason.'

'Kieron?' I say. The video is all fucked up. I see bare feds and Immigration officers on the walkway all round Kieron's door with Mandy and Ralph and the neighbours shouting abuse at them.

'They wanna send him to Rwanda or some shit,' Romy says.

'Where is he?'

'In his yard. He ain't letting them in and he ain't coming out.'

I look up and see Mandy and Ralph and half of what's left of Summerhouse crowded on the walkway.

Ralph is going into one, shouting at the feds, 'Why are you lot harassing hard-working, innocent people? You should be bloody ashamed of yourselves.'

I see Mandy approaching the feds. 'Excuse me,' she says. 'Who's in charge here?'

The feds ignore her.

Ralph is shouting, 'Immigration, they come round like stormtroopers. You'd think the dark side had won the war.'

Mandy keeps asking for who's in charge. 'I'd like to speak to the person in charge. Is that you?'

A fed says, 'Step back, please.'

Please? I hate the way the police pretend to be so polite. They put on this reasonable voice and say please. When a fed says please it doesn't have the same meaning as when you and me say it. What that fed is saying when he says please is that if you don't do what he tells you the next thing you know is you're gonna be on the floor with his knee on your neck.

I watch Mandy push past and go up to a fed outside Kieron's door.

'Excuse me,' she says. 'Are you in charge here?'

The fed says, 'You are obstructing police in the performance of their duties. Step back, please.'

Mandy doesn't move.

She says, 'I'm not obstructing you. I was born on this estate. I had my child on this estate. This is my home. All I'm asking is what's going on?'

'I need to clear the walkway,' the fed says. He raps Kieron's door. 'Could you open the door, please.'

Please? Go fuck yourself.

'You know the woman in that house is a cancer patient?' Mandy tells the fed. 'She's having chemo. She's very sick.'

The fed ignores Mandy and turns to the people behind her. 'Everyone off the walkway!' he shouts. 'Move back!'

Then Ralph shouts, 'You move back! This is our walkway.'

That gets everyone cheering and even I'm smiling. Ralph and his red face and grey hair going into one. I can see those wiry hairs he has coming out of his nostrils from here. He always make me laugh, Ralph. He never lets anyone in authority get away with anything. He knows how to stand up for himself.

More and more people are arriving in the courtyard. Bradders and Samsi are on the walkway and they're shouting at the feds. The top fed, the one Mandy is talking to, is trying to work out his next move. He was not expecting any of this. That's what happens when you come in Summerhouse when you're not wanted, you fucker.

The top fed turns to one of his men and says, 'All right. Get the donker.'

'What's a donker?' I ask Romy, who shrugs.

We don't have to wait no more than a minute to get the answer cos this fed steps up to the door and he's carrying this metal battering ram a couple of foot long. He swings it against the lock on the door.

Now everyone on the walkway is jeering and booing.

'Stormtroopers!' Ralph shouts. 'Bloody stormtroopers!'

Someone starts humming the tune from *Star Wars* whenever Darth Vader appears. Soon everyone's humming it. The fed takes a second swing at the door and it busts open.

'Fuck me,' Romy says as we watch a snatch squad dash inside Kieron's yard.

People are screaming and shouting. It's a madness.

Four feds drag Kieron outta the house onto the walkway. They've got his arms twisted up his back and his head pushed down.

The top fed says, 'Kieron Palmer, you're being detained by order of the Home Secretary.'

Diana comes out. She's crying, 'What's this about? Why are you doing this?'

A female fed says, 'The Home Secretary has signed an order for Kieron's immediate removal.'

'Nah, nah, nah,' Kieron says, though it ain't easy for him to speak with his head forced down like that and the feds twisting his arms. 'My mum sent so many letters to you lot. This is proper out of order.'

The feds are trying to clear a path so they can get Kieron down the stairs, across the courtyard and into the van. They're pushing people back.

Kieron shouts back to Diana, 'Mum, Mum. Don't worry. Remember to take your tablets, the right ones. I put them in the divider box. They're all laid out. Don't forget.'

'Get him down the stairs and into the van asap,' the top fed says.

Kieron is struggling all the way, and another fed has to join the four that are already on top of him so it takes five of the fuckers to get him to the stairs. All the time he's screaming and all the time Diana is crying and pleading.

I don't think I've ever seen anyone look as stunned as Diana is now. It's like the world just don't make sense to her no more.

Kieron keeps calling, 'Mum, Mum.'

I can hardly watch what I'm seeing. It's making me so upset and angry. I ain't even thinking about the heads or what Sully said about getting a crew down to the warehouse to clean up the mess before the feds find the lorry. All I can see is my guy Kieron getting hauled along the walkway to the stairs.

Some of the people on the walkway – and not just the youngers – they're angry like me and start getting in the feds' faces.

'Oi, man,' Mandy tells them, 'calm down. Don't give them no excuse to use violence.'

The top fed shouts, 'Get off the walkway. Move back. Everyone move back. Move back, madam.'

'I ain't moving back,' Mandy says to him. 'I'm staying right here. I'm within my rights.'

Ralph, who's next to her, chimes in, 'You show me where the law says I'm not allowed on my own walkway.'

Mandy says, 'Are you gonna fix that door that you just bust down?'

Diana is literally shaking. Ralph and some of the neighbours hurry over to comfort her. Seeing Kieron's mum in such a state just makes me more angry.

'Let's go,' I say to Romy and we run to the bottom of the stairs where Mandy comes down ahead of the feds hauling Kieron.

'They got no right to do this,' Mandy says to me. 'We can't let them take him. We ain't gonna let that happen. Come with me, Jaq,' she shouts. 'Everyone, come with me.'

Mandy walks over to where the police vans are all parked and she sits down in front of them. People follow her.

She looks over at me and shouts, 'Come, Jaq. We can stop them.'

One of the things about being a drug dealer is you like to keep a low profile. The last thing you want is to draw attention to yourself so I don't know about this.

Then the feds come out of the stairwell into the courtyard dragging Kieron.

'They're kidnapping man, this is a fucking kidnap,' Kieron shouts to everyone. Then he sees me and he says, 'Jaq, you believe this fuckery?'

As the feds drag him past, I say, 'Nah, not today, bruv. They ain't taking you. It ain't happening.'

I follow them as they load Kieron in the back of one of the vans.

'This is so fucked! Kieron, bruv. We'll figure this out. You ain't going nowhere. Love, bro, love.'

There's this sad look on Kieron's face when they load him in the van and close the doors.

That's when I decide. A'right, I'm a drug dealer and all my criminal instincts tell me not to get involved in some unnecessary beef with the feds. But this is different. This is my guy Kieron. Kieron's family. I turn to Romy, Bradders and Samsi. 'Come, we go.'

We run up to the front of the vans where Mandy's sitting. She gives me a big smile when I sit down next to her. She tells Romy and the youngers to go sit at the back so the feds don't try to reverse out.

'Keep it peaceful,' she says. 'Passive resistance. Don't give them no excuses.'

More and more people are joining the sit-down. The

top fed is looking like what the fuck? Like what am I supposed to do now?

These two feds come up and pull Mandy up by the arms. But as soon as they get her out of the way, two more people come and take her place. When the feds turn to deal with them, Mandy jumps back in her place next to me.

'Jaq,' she says, 'do you think you can get more people down here? The more numbers we have, the better.'

I get my phone out and start scrolling through my contacts.

'But tell them to keep it cool, yeah? No violence. This is a peaceful protest. Tell them to spread the word.'

I'm sending out messages when Mandy starts chanting, 'Let him go! Let him go!'

Everyone joins in. Wow. Hearing that. Hearing all these people chanting together. The hairs on my arms stand up. I get proper goosebumps.

Everyone's chanting, 'Let him go!'

I never felt before what I am feeling now. And I don't really know why.

Let him go! Let him go!

'These vans ain't going nowhere,' Mandy says.

She gives me a smile and squeezes my hand. It's like the feeling I got when Dris and me sat on the low wall together all those years ago.

Like belonging.

LET HIM GO!

It's getting on for six o'clock and now there's a couple of hundred or more people sitting all round the vans. Summerhouse ain't been this mobbed ever. The feds start beeping their horns and roaring their engines, trying to intimidate us.

Let him go! Let him go!

No one moves. Kieron ain't going nowhere.

From time to time, the feds dive in and drag someone away. But all it does is open up a spot for someone else to jump in. The top fed shouts through a megaphone and says if we don't move we'll all be arrested, but everyone just boos him or shouts back, 'Go on, then!'

He looks proper stressed. Welcome to Summerhouse.

Ralph comes up. 'Where do you want me, Mand?' he says.

Some of the women make some very explicit suggestions.

'You lot have got filthy minds,' he says, laughing. 'I thought this was a decent protest.'

Ralph is probably blushing except you can't tell cos his face is so red already.

People are handing out sandwiches and cake and teas. The youngers are ordering up food on Uber and Deliveroo.

Erin, Mandy and Dris's daughter, comes up with some of her schoolfriends. Mandy waves her over.

'You got your new glasses,' she says.

'Do you like them?' Erin asks.

'They make you look very intellectual. I bet one day you're going to write a book.'

Erin and her friends pass round crisps and sweets. Erin offers me some chocolate. She knows me by sight but we ain't ever talked. She's got a sweet smile. She ain't one of these cheeky kids. Dris brought her up proper. But I'm feeling a little bit awkward because of what went down with Dris and all the time I'm wondering what does Erin know?

'How did you know about the protest?' Mandy asks her.

'Mum, are you kidding? It's all over social media. Everyone knows about it.'

Mandy leans past Erin to talk to me. 'Jaq, go get that lot over there and tell them to come in closer. Anyone who's up for it, get them sitting in front of the vans.'

I'm glad to get away cos I am not comfortable being round Erin, especially as she's being so nice. Dris broke the code. No question about that. And he deserved what he got. But Erin didn't do anything wrong and she lost her dad. And no little girl deserves that. Suddenly, I'm thinking about my own dad and how I ain't seen him for about five years. He could be dead for all I know. I hope he ain't cos when I close my eyes the way I do when the pictures come and tell me what I really want, I can see my dad waiting for me. He's alone by a wall under a street-light, waiting. And I see me walking towards him and him not recognising me at first. But then he sees it's me and this big smile breaks out all over his face and he hugs and kisses me and says, 'Jaq, I've missed you so much.'

No little girl deserves to lose her dad. Don't matter what he did.

So I get up and make my way over to a group that are hanging round and don't seem to know what to do. I tell them we need all the bodies we can get and for them to go over and sit some of them in front of the vans and some behind.

The top fed is trying to keep his cool but he's getting more and more frustrated.

I look at my phone and see a text from Sharon: whats going on?

I do not know what to say to her. Cos I don't know what's going on. Yes, I want the Dickie Simms ting but I've also got this situation going on with Kieron. I should probably text back but I don't.

I hear someone calling my name. I look round and see Dushane across the courtyard. Dushane. What the fuck? I ain't seen him since Sully stuck the strap in his face and told him he was stepping down. He's waving to me to come over like he's still top boy. But I ain't sure if I should go. I mean, what would Sully say if he saw me talking to man? But Dushane keeps waving at me so eventually I go over.

'What the fuck are you doing?' he says.

'Immigration's kidnapped Kieron, innit.'

'What? And youse think this is a good idea? Bringing all these feds into the ends?'

'No offence, Dushane. But what's man supposed to do here? Let the feds just take the brother?'

'How are we supposed to do business with all this going on?'

'It's Kieron, man. We gotta stop this.'

'Nah,' he says. 'What you gotta do is sell. That's your job.'

The brother has changed. He used to be so cool. Always still when everyone else was jumping around. Always in control of himself. In all those early years I never saw Dushane looking concerned about anything. Even when there was a lotta shit going on, Dushane was calm. He ain't that guy now. I wouldn't say he looks desperate. I wouldn't use that word exactly. But he ain't still now. He's twitchy. There's something ragged about him now. He's trying to give orders like he was still top boy, but he ain't in control now. Not of the mandem and maybe not even of himself.

'Bruv,' I tell him, 'I'm staying here.'

This angry look comes into his eyes, but before he can say anything a policewoman comes up and says to him, 'Move out of the way, please, sir.'

Please? Sir?

'Fuck off,' I say. 'Go on, fuck off.'

Mandy has been watching and she signals me to keep calm and mind my language.

'Sir?' the policewoman says.

'A'right,' Dushane says and steps back.

Dushane keeps a low profile. He don't like to draw attention so he's happy to step back.

'You too, miss,' the fed says.

'Nah,' I tell her. 'My friend's in that van. I ain't going nowhere.'

Dushane looks at me, shaking his head. He don't like

this at all. But I don't care. He ain't top boy no more. Nothing he can do. I watch him walk away, and for the first time in my life it hits me that there's something pathetic about man. Like here we are all together, all this positive energy, and there he is, slipping away, alone.

And then I feel bad about dissing man, even to myself. Dushane told me this story one time about his dad. His dad's name is Wendell. Wendell left home when Dushane was five or six and Dushane only saw him a couple of times after that. The last time he saw him was when he accidentally bumped into him in the street, innit. It was during the Bobby Raikes and Lee Greene ting, and him and Sully had some business they had to do when Dushane spies someone he recognises, more from the pictures his mum kept in a drawer than from his own memory. So he goes over and he says, 'Wagwan, Wendell.' Wendell is with a little kid, Jason, and he tells Dushane that Jason's his son and he has another boy and a girl, twins. Dushane says to Jason, don't be shy, that he's his brother, and then he goes back to Sully who's waiting for him on the corner.

'Who was that?' Sully asked.

'Nobody,' Dushane said.

When Dushane told me that I almost put my hand on his arm. I didn't. Of course I didn't. If I had, Dushane would of looked at me as if there was something wrong with me. But I did feel kind of sad for him. No son should ever have to call his dad a nobody, cos that's what Dushane was saying with that. Maybe that's what was hanging over Dushane since he was a kid, his dad being a nobody. Maybe that's why he did what he did to be top boy. So he wouldn't get called a nobody.

He ain't even there to see Shelley arrive with Naomi.

Mandy jumps up and gives them hugs. 'Babes, you came!'

I have to laugh cos Shelley and Naomi are looking at the whole madness and they don't know what to think of it. They ain't ever been on a protest before ever. But then neither have I. Neither has anyone here today, except maybe Mandy. I'm hearing when she was in the pen she organised a lotta protests at conditions and that.

Let him go! Let him go!

I'm going back to sit in front of the vans when Romy suddenly scuttles under the van they put Kieron in. Everyone cheers. A couple of feds try to catch a foot or an arm and drag him out but Romy's too quick for them and they don't wanna go under the van and get dirty.

Then Bradders and some youngers lie down right in front of the wheels of Kieron's van. Bradders sparks up a zoot. Two feds pull him up and push him away. Bradders looks like he might start swinging.

'Brad!' I shout, 'Allow it, man! Mandy says passive resistance, innit.'

Samsi's filming the whole thing. 'I've got that on IG LIVE, bro,' she tells one of the feds pushing Bradders.

'Stop filming me,' the fed shouts at her. Then he turns to Bradders and says, 'And put that out.'

'Nah, cuz. I'm here to film all your fuckery and the only way you're gonna stop me filming is if you pattern yourself out of here, cuz,' she says.

By now there's three or four hundred people. Maybe more. It's hard to count. But more people are arriving every minute.

Mandy leads Shelley and Naomi over to the front of the van where Erin is sitting.

'Look at Erin and her glasses. You look so mature,' Naomi says.

'What do you want us to do?' Shelley asks.

'Sit down,' Mandy says. 'And remember. No violence. And no cussing these dickhead feds. I don't wanna hear no rassclaat bad language, get me?'

Everyone's laughing.

The top fed comes over to Mandy. 'This is obstruction and you will be arrested unless you disperse and go home.'

'We are home,' Mandy says. 'What makes you think you can just drag a member of our community from his house and send him to a whole country he doesn't know? What kind of madness is that? How do you sleep at night?'

The top fed gives up and climbs into one of the vehicles. I see him get on the radio.

Ralph's partner Arthur comes down with two folding chairs.

'What are you doing, you mad old bastard?' Ralph says.

'I haven't sat on the floor since I was a hippie in the sixties,' Arthur says. 'Besides, sitting on the road is very unhygienic. You've got no idea what germs you're catching.'

Arthur sets out the two chairs and then produces a bottle of gin, a bottle of tonic and plastic cups which he hands out.

'Can I have one of them?'

It's Stef.

'No, son. The police would nick me for giving alcohol to a minor,' Arthur says.

Erin calls Stef over and makes space for him. 'How do you like my glasses?' she asks.

'Yeah, they're cool, innit,' Stef says.

'They're like the ones my dad used to wear. I asked for

them specially. The optician says I probably got my bad eyesight from my dad. You're lucky you got good eyesight.'

'Yeah,' Stef says.

Erin is doing all the work. Nothing from Stefan.

'Cool chain,' she says.

'It's Jamie's.'

'Do you know Kieron?'

'Who?'

'The boy in the van. The Immigration took him.'

Let him go! Let him go!

Stef and Erin join in the chant. They're looking at each other shyly. Definitely something going on here. Erin's friends are singing along to TikToks on their phones.

The top fed climbs out of the van. He looks very tired. He nods to a fed who opens up the back of the van. I'm watching carefully. I'm puzzled. What's going on?

Then Kieron appears at the back of the van. He's looking tentative and confused.

The top fed shouts out, 'The Home Office has decided to release Mr Palmer.'

The whole of Summerhouse erupts into a roar.

Kieron steps out. He's mobbed. I push my way through and give him a massive hug.

'You all right, bro?' I say.

'I'm good, my fam,' he says.

There's tears in his eyes. Diana comes up. Now everyone is jumping up and down. We hardly even notice the police getting back in their vans and driving off.

'Mandy, that was mad. Thank you, cuz,' Kieron says.

'Jaq!'

Mandy grabs my arm and holds it up like I'm a heavyweight champ.

‘That was special,’ Mandy says.

The two of us are so happy, we throw our arms round each other. Someone I don’t know takes a photo of me and Mandy, like that, big smiles, our fists in the air like we’d just won the World Cup.

They let him go.

Summerhouse 1 Home Office 0.

SHARON THE FED (AGAIN)

Sharon is doing her nut. She's been texting me non-stop. But the day I've had, starting with Lauryn, then the heads in the boxes, then the Irish, then the whole Kieron Immigration thing, I ain't had a chance to think about Sharon and Dickie Simms' stash.

Before I leave Summerhouse, I tell Romy to get a crew together and go and clean up the mess at the warehouse and get rid of the heads. I text Sully to see if he needs me for anything. He texts back so at least I know the Irish ain't got to him, at least not yet. He says he don't need me though. I don't know what he's got planned but I know he'll have something cos Sully ain't gonna let nobody steal his grub.

By the time I show up to meet Sharon it's late and she is not happy, and when she's not happy I see this different side of her, the cop side. Like I'm the one in the wrong and I gotta explain myself, cos if I don't, I'm in trouble. It fucks me off.

'I need to know if you're serious about this,' she says in

her cop voice. 'If I can't rely on you, I need to know now and find someone else.'

'I'm serious,' I tell her. 'What's the issue here?'

'The issue here, Jaq, is that we're hearing the shipment is on its way. It's going to be arriving in the next few days and it's not going to be at the address for long. Couple of days at the most. I explained this to you.'

'And I heard you.'

'Good to know,' the sarky bitch says and I almost walk away right then. 'So. Question for you. When are you proposing to do this?'

'This Dickie Simms, is he Irish?'

'No, English. Why?'

'Nothing,' I say.

It just jumped into my head that maybe this Dickie Simms is connected with the Irish fella on the phone.

'What's that got to do with when you're going to do it?'

I really don't like her cop voice and it's getting a lot stronger now.

'I told you nothing,' I tell her. 'I was just asking.'

'So when can you do it?'

'Firstly, I need the address. The exact address.'

Sharon hesitates a second. 'If I tell you, I need a guarantee that you won't just take it and try to cut me out.'

I wanna punch her in her stupid cop face.

'If you don't tell me where it is, how am I supposed to get the stash? I need to know where it is. I need to know is it a flat? Is it a house? What is it?'

'It's a shop,' she says, after thinking about whether to tell me or not for like a minute.

'What kind of shop?'

'An estate agent.'

'A'right. Where?'

She licks her lips like she's about to tell me the biggest secret in the world. 'It's on Kilburn High Road.'

I don't like having to drag this out of her. I don't like her attitude and she don't like mine, which ain't exactly useful when you're planning to rob a gangster's stash together.

So I say, 'Sharon, we need to clear the air here. Cos if we don't trust each other at this stage it's hard to see how we can do this thing. Cos once it's done, it's done, and there's a mutual destruct button. I can bring you down and you can bring me down. All it takes is one phone call to the feds. I don't want that to happen and I'm assuming you don't want that to happen either.'

'No, I don't,' she says. 'No way.'

'Just talking about this, we're already conspiring to commit a crime, right?'

'Conspiracy to rob, yes. You can get seven years.'

'So we've already crossed the line just by having this conversation. Question is, are we gonna go through with this?'

'I hope so. It's a lot of money.'

'Me too,' I say. 'So we have to trust each other.'

'Listen, Jaq, I'm sorry. It's just this is right out of my comfort zone and I'm a cautious person, that's my nature. So I'm sorry if I pissed you off. I hope we can move forward.'

'We can,' I say. 'But you gotta let me do my thing the way I do it.'

'I understand. I will. Just tell me what you need.'

'The exact address for starters.'

She shows me on her phone. Her smartphone, not the burner.

'How soon after it arrives will you know it's in there?' I ask.

'The CI says he'll know as soon as it's in the shop.'

'And he'll tell you?'

'Correct. So we'll know within minutes.'

'And it's gonna be in there how long?'

'At least two days, maybe more. But then Dickie's going to move it.'

I smile at her. 'No, he ain't. Cos we're moving it first.'

Sharon grins, a lot more relaxed now. But I'm bullshitting here, stunting, cos I don't know if my man Kieron is gonna be able to do this after what happened today with the Immigration. I'm gonna have to figure this out.

'I'll text you as soon as I know it's arrived,' Sharon says.

'Cool,' I say.

Driving home, I call Kieron.

'How you doing, bruv?' he says.

'I'm good, yeah. How about you?'

'Mum's totally freaked, innit,' he says. 'They bust the door down and we can't get anyone to come and fix it till tomorrow and she's worried in case we get robbed or they come back again.'

'You need to talk to your solicitor, bruv,' I say.

'Yeah, yeah. I'm doing that tomorrow.'

'Listen, bruv. This other ting. How you feeling about that?'

Kieron don't say nothing for a few moments.

'What do you think?' I say. 'It's a big opportunity.'

'Yeah,' he says. 'Massive.'

'You still on for it?'

'Yeah, bruv, yeah.'

But his voice don't sound like he's on for it at all.

'Cos the thing we're waiting on, it's gonna be there soon, which means we gotta be ready to move fast. Can you do that?'

'Yeah, I can do that,' he says.

'I don't wanna push you to do something you don't wanna do.'

'Nah, I wanna.'

'A'right. I'll see you tomorrow. Love.'

'Love, bro. Love.'

When I hang up I go over every word he said and the tone he said it. And I'm thinking, he ain't gonna do this. So what the fuck do I do? I remember what Jimmy the Indian used to tell me about when you have options. You list the candidate moves like a chess player and then you pick the best one.

Here's my candidates:

One, try and persuade Kieron to do it.

Two, ditch Kieron and go to Romy.

Three, do it myself.

Four, forget all about Dickie Simms and the five to seven mil's worth of drugs that's arriving in that estate agent's on Kilburn High Road.

I'm still going over the candidates when I park the car outside my yard. I let myself in and I hear the baby. He ain't crying exactly, more kind of burbling a little. Then I see Lauryn fast asleep under a blanket on the sofa.

'Aw, did Mummy fall asleep?' I say to the baby.

Lauryn is really gonna have to pick a name for him. I'm gonna tell her tomorrow. The baby's fine. He ain't stinky and he looks happy enough. Lauryn still ain't woken up. Then I see something on the blanket. I can't believe my eyes. It's like a knife in my heart. I put the baby down and pick up a silver wrap. I sniff it. It's what I thought it was. Dark.

Lauryn breathes in heavy and opens her eyes.

I hide the tinfoil in my hand and smile at her.

'How was your day?' I say.

LAURYN'S DAY OUT

Lauryn is still asleep when I leave the house. I cut across Summerhouse on my way to the Number One Caff to see Sully and there's a family, white people, hauling their shit to a removal van. They ain't even fully out the door when the orange grilles go up over the door and windows. Summerhouse is getting more empty by the day.

I'm taking the shortcut through the courtyard when I see it. Fuck me. It's a fucking mural of me and Mandy. Someone's copied the photo of us after they let Kieron go. I stop to look at it. I like it, can't lie. Even though I know Sully ain't gonna like it. I mean, you can't draw attention to yourself in this game and, fuck me, is this drawing attention.

Ralph comes past. 'Good likeness,' he says.

I just shrug.

He waves a letter in my face. 'The postman gave me this just now. Another threatening letter from the landlords. I have to vacate my home – my *home* – by the end of the month, and if I don't, they're saying I will have made myself voluntarily homeless and the council will have no responsibility to rehouse me. It's a liberty. It's ethnic cleansing, that's what it is. They're ethnically cleansing poor people. They don't want ordinary working-class people living here. They want us out where they can't see us and they are using every dirty trick in the book to get us out. *Accidentally* turning the water off. *Accidentally* causing the gas and electric to go off. Not fixing the lifts. And then these' – he waves the letter angrily – 'threatening letters. It's a crime to send threatening letters. The landlords should be in jail.'

I like Ralph, but when he goes into one of his rants, the best thing to do, I've learned from experience, is to just nod and try and escape quick as you can. If you engage, you'll never get away. I agree with every word he was saying but I couldn't tell him that or I would be here until Christmas. So I nod and say for real and start to move off.

'Well done, Jaq,' he says. 'What you and Mandy did yesterday, stopping the Immigration and police, that was how we fight back. Together. If only the little people would understand that – that if we stand together, we ain't little no more. We're big. Bigger than them, anyway. They're nothing but bullies.'

'Yeah, yeah, for real,' I say, making my escape.

'You should be proud of yourself,' I hear him saying, still ranting. 'You and Mandy both.'

I'm coming out of the estate when two young girls see me – I don't know them – and they come up and ask for selfies with me. They're so excited that I forget my criminal instincts and pose with them. They were on the protest and they're telling me how inspiring it was and how amazing I am. It's kind of nice to hear but it ain't the reality.

'It weren't really me,' I tell them. 'It was the other girl, Mandy. She started it. All I did was join in.'

'But when you said to all them people, go sit here, go sit there, they all did what you said,' one of the girls says. 'You've got power!'

'You were showing people what to do and they listened to you,' the other girl says.

'You're like an influencer,' the first girl says.

'I ain't an influencer,' I say. 'I ain't anything. Take care.'

I hurry on cos Sully don't like to be kept waiting. But when I get to the Number One Caff I look in the window and Sully's in there at a table talking to Dushane. Looks like a serious talk. I'm wondering if Sully has changed his mind and is talking to Dushane about the heads and the problem with the Irish.

I wait outside.

An old boy walks past and he nods at me and gives me a wink. 'Well done,' he says.

Talk about drawing attention to yourself. Fuck me.

Eventually, Sully comes out.

'Wagwan,' I say.

'Wagwan,' he says. 'Did you get a crew down to the shop to clean up that mess?'

'Yeah, it's done,' I tell him. 'Romy done it, innit. Listen, do you need me for this ting with the Irish today?'

'Why?'

'It's just Lauryn ain't right. Last night I found this.' I show him the tinfoil wrap.

'That ain't good,' he says.

Sully don't react in a big way to anything, so when he says something ain't good, what he's really saying is you've got a big problem here that you need to take care of.

'She ain't been outta the house since the whole Curtis ting, apart from the hospital, and I need to spend a bit of time with her.'

'How long has she been using?'

'Not long. Definitely not when she was pregnant or they would of picked it up at the hospital.'

'How's she look?'

'Tired. But not like a nittie or nothing.'

'A'right,' he says.

'It's just I told Kieron to stay at home for a bit. After the Immigration ting, man needs to be careful. But obviously if you need me for the Irish, I'm here for you.'

'It's cool.'

'You sure?'

'You take care of Lauryn.'

There's something in the way Sully's talking that makes me think things ain't as cool and under control as he's making out. So I ask him again about the Irish.

'I told you it's cool,' he says. His tone is sharp. He don't wanna be asked no more about this so I leave it and go.

What I found out later was that Sully tried to switch off one of the Irish the night before. Somewhere a long way from the ends, up country somewhere. It didn't go according to plan and instead one of Sully's guys got shot in the head.

I go back to mine and Lauryn is in the kitchen with Becks who's trying to persuade her to go to some yoga class.

'It'll do you good, babes,' Becks says.

But Lauryn's being all moody and saying she don't wanna go.

'My trainer Gerry always says that exercise is good for the vanity and good for the sanity,' Becks says.

'Come with me then,' Lauryn says.

'I'd love to,' Becks says, 'but I have back-to-back Zooms and calls. It's a nightmare.'

'I'll go with you,' I jump in.

It takes another twenty minutes, but eventually Lauryn gives in and that's how we end up at a fucking yoga class specially for new mums trying to get their bodies back in shape. To be honest, it's got its compensations. There are some nice-looking new mums in there. And some of them are definitely looking back at me.

Lauryn does not wanna be here. When the teacher shows her how to warm up, Lauryn turns to her and says, 'I'm not gonna do anything that's gonna make me sweat.'

I nearly bust out laughing. So Lauryn. The teacher just looks at her like she's got a right one here.

I take a seat and start texting while watching out of the corner of my eye the women doing their downward dog and cobra and whatever. The teacher says something about cat cow or cow cat or something like that and they're on all fours and arching their backs. I like watching that, can't lie. There's this one woman, she's white, and she looks over at me more than once. I go back to texting but every now and then I check on her.

Lauryn comes over and says, 'I've had enough.'

'Can't we stay a bit longer?' I say, and I nod discreetly at the woman I've been watching.

'I thought we were here for me?' Lauryn says.

'We are.'

'Then let's go.'

The teacher crosses over, looking a bit concerned. 'It's beneficial if you finish the class,' she says.

'Sorry, hon, but I'm just not feeling it,' Lauryn says.

As she's collecting her things, one of the new mums comes up shyly.

'I hope you don't mind,' she says. 'But you're that girl, aren't you?'

'Depends what girl you're referring to,' I say. I'm already suspicious here. What fucking girl?

'From that estate?'

Her friend, the nice-looking one who's been giving me the eye, comes over. 'Summerhouse,' she says.

'That's the one,' the first girl says. 'The protest. It's you, isn't it?'

'Nah,' I say. 'You got me mixed up with someone else.'

'Yeah, it's her,' Lauryn says.

I give her a look, like shut up.

The woman gets out her phone and shows me the photo of me and Mandy. It's all over social media.

'What an amazing picture,' she says. 'You and that other girl look so strong. It's so inspiring.'

I'm feeling kind of flattered but, fuck me, no. I can't have my picture out there like this. The only reason I'm thinking Sully ain't been on at me is cos he's got bigger problems to deal with right now with the Irish and that. But sooner or later he's gonna hear about all this and then he's gonna be very pissed off.

'Anyway, well done,' the woman says and there's this twinkle in her eye.

'Thank you,' I say.

As me and Lauryn are leaving, I hear one of them say to the other, 'Told you it was her.'

I turn round and see them looking at her phone and the other new mums and even the teacher are all gathering round asking what's going on.

Lauryn says to me, 'You could get so many followers if you post that picture on your Insta. Seriously, you could monetise it.'

'Yeah, just what I need.'

We go to a cafe across the street and grab a couple of coffees and sit at a table by the window. I'm dreading having the conversation I'm gonna have to have so I chat shit for a bit.

'Listen,' I say, 'the yoga, you should stick with that class. It'd be good for you.'

'Nah, it ain't for me,' she says.

I can't put it off no more. I take the tinfoil wrap outta my pocket and put it on the table in front of her.

'Why don't you tell me what this is?'

'Cos I got no idea what you're on about.'

OK, she's gonna play dumb.

'Is that right?' I say.

'People are looking,' she says. 'Put it away.'

'Thought you didn't know what it was?'

'I don't.'

'Where did you get it from?'

'People are looking. What's wrong with you?'

'You know this fucks you up, right?'

'Why are you talking to me like I'm some kind of crack-head with no front teeth?'

'Cos you're my sister and this is dark. I seen enough people get fucked up by this and I don't wanna see the same ting happen to you. So this ain't happening no more, a'right?'

'A'right, a'right,' she says quickly. 'I won't do it no more. Just put it away.'

I pick up the wrap and put it in my pocket.

'Look,' she says, 'I ain't addicted or nothing. I just needed to take the edge off. It's been hard, Jaq, with the baby and everything that happened with . . .'

I give her a look and she stops before she says the name that I don't allow to be said out loud.

'It's been hard,' she says, kind of quiet.

'You know what? Let's have a family day, yeah? Let's get little man and spend it together.'

'You got the time?'

'For you? Yeah, always.'

JIMMY THE INDIAN

We're heading home to pick up the baby when this black Audi races through the bus lane just as this man in a three-piece suit, shirt and tie and polished brogues is crossing the road. The man curses the driver and waves his hands. The driver slams on the brakes and reverses almost right up to the fella and jumps outta the car. Big white guy, shaved head, tattoos on his neck and arms. Are there women who go for that look? There must be, but I don't understand why.

The driver comes up to the man he nearly killed and shouts in his face, 'Shut up, you fucking Paki.'

'I'll show you a fucking Paki,' the well-dressed fella says and he throws a punch that sends the driver staggering into the back of his own car.

One punch. He's squaring up getting ready to hit him again but he don't have to. The driver is sliding to the ground. His senses are gone, he don't know what day it is.

The well-dressed guy is standing over him, his fists ready in case the driver gets up again. But that ain't gonna happen.

'Look who it ain't,' Lauryn says.

I look at the fella. He's stocky but not fat, sort of squarish. His black hair is going grey and his face is kind of rough-looking. It's him. I can't believe my eyes.

Jimmy the Indian.

He's twisting these big gold rings on his right hand.

'Fuck me,' I say.

Jimmy is already straightening his tie and starting to walk away when me and Lauryn hurry up to him. Jimmy doesn't recognise us at first, but when he does he flashes a massive smile with these massive extra-white teeth that don't look real.

'My guy didn't know who he was racially abusing,' I say, looking at the driver, who is having a lot of trouble getting to his feet.

Jimmy shouts, 'My god, my god! There's too much beauty here, I have to shield my eyes.' And he puts a hand over his eyes all dramatic. 'It's too much! My eyes, my eyes! They're burning.'

He grabs the two of us, one in each arm, and pulls us in for a hug. He moves his arms to our shoulders and steers us away from the driver, who's trying to get into his car except he can't find the door. People are laughing at him and some kid is videoing him on his phone.

Jimmy looks at us all serious, taking us in.

'What a pleasure it is to see you girls,' he says. 'How long has it been?'

It's been a lotta years, can't lie. Jimmy goes on about how amazing we are and how beautiful we are. I tell him Lauryn's got a baby and he wants to know everything about the baby and who the dad is. That's when the conversation goes a little quiet. But Jimmy's a very intelligent man, very sensitive, and he don't press the point about the babyfather.

'Speaking of dads,' he says, 'you know, I saw your dad.'

'When?' I ask.

'It was about two months ago, two, three months.'

'Where's he living now?' I ask.

'He's in Canada.'

'Canada?'

'Toronto. I was over there for a business meeting, and I'm in a restaurant in company and this fella comes in and sits at the next table. I'm not looking at him but then I hear the voice and I go, that's Vincent. And I look over and it's him. We had a big catch-up that night. He was asking about both you girls. But I had to tell him that I hadn't seen you in yonks. Said how much he missed you, how proud he was of you.'

'Yeah, course he did,' Lauryn says, sarky like.

'He did, he really did. I had a long talk with him, and to be frank I thought he seemed sad.'

'Sad? Like what do you mean?' I ask.

'Sad about the way his life has turned out.'

'I'll bet,' Lauryn says. 'Does he have a family over there? I'll bet he does.'

'Be honest with you, Lauryn, I don't know.'

'I thought you had a big catch-up with him?' Lauryn says like she's catching him out in a lie.

'It was more about the business side of things,' Jimmy says.

I know he ain't telling the whole truth here and probably Dad did have another family. Just like Dushane's dad Wendell.

'Do you have a number for him or anything?' I ask.

'You know what,' Jimmy says, 'it's in my other phone which I've left in the house.'

I give Jimmy my number and make him promise to send me Dad's number. Jimmy straightens his tie and smiles. If anything's blinding here, it's Jimmy's teeth. I didn't know anything could be that white. He hugs us both and tells us he's gonna remember this day for the rest of his life and promises we'll keep in touch. He crosses the road and goes off.

'Notice how he didn't ask about Mum,' I say.

Lauryn laughs. 'Did you really see him and Mum doing it?'

'I swear down,' I say. 'But I notice he didn't say anything about her.'

'You blame him?'

If Jimmy did have a thing with Mum, the last thing he would want is to start that up again, I'm thinking. Mum's a disaster. Jimmy would not want to get involved. Unless of course he's still seeing her. Me and Lauryn wouldn't know. We ain't seen Mum in a long time either.

'Why do you want Dad's number?' Lauryn asks.

I shrug. 'Ain't you curious about him?'

'Nah,' Lauryn says. 'I never think about him. Do you?'

'Can't lie,' I say. 'I do.'

'Why?'

'Cos he's my dad, innit. He's blood. And one of these days, yeah, I'd like to see him again.'

'I wouldn't.'

'You're you, I'm me.'

We go home to pick up the baby, who's looking unhappy and kicking his little legs. Becks is on the phone to one of her clients and is looking frantic so she's very relieved to see us cos it's been longer than what she was expecting. We grab the pram and the baby things and head out to the market.

I buy a teddy bear from a stall. I show it to the baby and pretend like it's talking.

'Hello, little boy with no name. Can I come and sit with you in your pram?' I say in a silly voice.

But the baby has no fucking idea what I'm on about and ain't interested in the teddy. I don't think they get interested in that kind of stuff till they're older.

'You're gonna have to think of a name for him,' I tell Lauryn.

'Yeah, yeah.'

'Look!'

There's a stall with name plaques for kids' bedrooms. I drag Lauryn up to it and we stare at the names.

'Which one do you like?' I ask her.

'I dunno.'

'Come on, we need to get cracking.'

'It's hard.'

'What about that one – Hank?'

We both crack up.

'What about Delroy? Likkle baby Delroy.'

'No!'

'What about Bunny, like after Mum's brother that she never saw? Always thought that was a weird fucking name.'

'Weren't he a paedo?'

'Nah, he was just a pervert. Mum said he used to watch her through the cloudy window in the shower.'

'That's gross.'

'We're going to the canal now, Delroy,' I say to the baby.

'Don't call him that.'

It's a beautiful day. Young people are sitting out at the bars and cafes along the towpath, chatting and laughing. I recognise one or two of my customers from back in the day when I was a soldier on the corners. They recognise me too, or think they do, and sort of half smile.

'I'm proud of you, innit,' I say to Lauryn. 'It's a lot what you went through and look at us now. Me, you, the little king in there. We're a family. People would kill for this.'

'I literally did,' Lauryn says.

'I told you. That never happened.'

'But it did, Jaq. I appreciate what you're doing for me, but it happened. If it hadn't of happened, we wouldn't be here right now. We wouldn't have this.'

'Well, then, we have to cherish it still.'

Lauryn don't look convinced.

'One last place I wanna take you,' I say and link her arm.

'Where?' she says. 'I'm tired after all that yoga. I wanna go home.'

'You're coming with me. Someone we gotta see, innit.'

When we get to the nail bar, Shelley ain't there. Just Mandy doing reception and Naomi with a client. They squeal with delight when they see us and jump up and hug us both.

'Did you see the mural they did of us?' Mandy says.

'I saw it,' I say. 'It's kind of hard, still.'

'Although I think whoever painted it made me look bigger than what I am in reality, to be fair.'

'That's true,' Naomi says.

Then Shelley appears, coming out of the back office. She's almost crying she's so pleased to see Lauryn and gives her a big kiss. They all crowd round the pram and lift up the little king so they can admire him.

'Aw, isn't he cute,' Shelley says. 'So cute. He's beautiful.'

I see this look come into Lauryn's eyes. Any time anyone says the baby's beautiful it sets her mind off in a certain direction where it bumps up against Curtis. She's obsessed that maybe the baby looks more like him than it does her. But she manages a smile.

'Do you really think so?' she says.

Shelley gives her a look like what's wrong with you? Like why aren't you like all the other new mums who think their baby is the most beautiful baby that's ever been born?

'What?' Shelley says. 'Are you joking? Or course he is. What's his name?'

'Delroy,' I say.

'It's not,' Lauryn says. 'Don't listen to her. I just haven't been able to think of one yet.'

The baby starts to cry.

'Too much female attention?' Naomi says.

'There ain't no such ting as too much female attention,' I say. 'Anyway we was just passing and thought we'd pop in.'

'Oh no,' Shelley says. 'You're not going.'

I try to go to the door but it would be easier to escape from Ralph. Shelley grabs my arm and says, 'No, it's not a question. You. Are. Not. Going. Sit down.'

She steers me to a chair and pushes me into it.

'Jaq, there's something Naomi has been dying to do for you for a long time.'

'I'm definitely interested in that.'

Naomi sits across the table from me and takes my hands.

'Shut up,' Lauryn says. 'You've got a partner, a very beautiful one.'

'I ain't never fucked with shit like this before,' I say.

'It's about time you got them wonky little claw toes sorted out and all,' Lauryn says, as she settles in for her treatment.

She's had this done a million times and she's comfortable. I ain't never had it done and I ain't comfortable at all. I never let anyone take hold of my hand less it's a girlfriend. It's too intimate. And even though I know Naomi a bit and she's a nice woman, it's not easy. I'm also wondering why anybody would do this for a job? I mean, seriously? What the fuck's in it for them? Having to deal with someone's hands when you don't know where they've been. And that's before they even have to do the feet. I don't even want to think about that. But it's kind of funny. After a bit, I start to relax and let Naomi get on with it. It starts to feel nice.

Naomi says, 'You hear about the chain Shelley's buying? It's gonna be called Shelley's. Just that, just Shelley's. Drop the nail bar. Sounds more confident, you know?'

'Chain? Serious?' Lauryn says.

'I spotted this opportunity,' Shelley says. 'It's perfect.'

'And it's the right time,' Naomi says. She's even more excited than Shelley. 'You see the way the beauty business is going now? Everyone wants to look their best and they will spend money to achieve that.'

Shelley looks at Lauryn direct in the eye. 'So are you gonna come and get involved cos Shelley's is going places. You already know the dream.'

'I've got the baby, Shell,' Lauryn says.

'I'm not saying right now. When you're ready. Whenever. You're family.'

There's a tear in Lauryn's eye. 'I appreciate it, sis,' she says. 'I really do.'

'Offer will always stand, babe.'

Shelley won't take any money. I knew she wouldn't. Leaving the shop, I examine my nails. They look good, can't lie.

On the way home, Lauryn tells me this is the best day out she's ever had. All that time I'm with Lauryn I don't think once about all the shit I usually have to think about cos of the line of business I'm in. I don't think about the heads in the van or the Irish and the missing food. I don't think about Sharon and Dickie Simms. I don't even think about Kieron, Kieron's family. I don't look at my phone once, and for a drug dealer, that don't happen a lot.

Nah, I just feel chill and a little bit giggly and silly being with my sister. Seeing her smile makes me happy.

COME BACK

Becks makes a big fuss of our nails and tries to sell me the idea of going for a pedicure together sometime. I tell her I'll think about it. She says she needs to have a night out. I don't really wanna go out, but Becks has been on Zooms all day and she's stir crazy. So I go and get changed and make myself look nice. Or even nicer, I should say.

When I come downstairs Lauryn's taking selfies for her socials, taking pictures of her manicure, glass of wine in her hand. The baby is on the floor on his play mat. He's happy. We're all happy.

'You don't mind me going out?' I say.

'Of course not,' Lauryn says. 'Don't worry. I can watch a film with the little king, whatever.'

'But I said the whole day would be a family day. For you and me.'

'Today has been amazing,' she says. 'I even got a job. Me and Shelley. It's meant to be. Go be with your woman. It's cool.'

'A'right,' I say, 'have one of your fancy baths and get to bed.'

I give Lauryn a kiss and she says, 'I love you, Jaq.'

'I love you too, babes.'

'No. Jaq,' she says, all serious. 'I mean I really love you. You're the best sister in the world. All the times you've been there for me. I can't even count them. You're amazing.'

'I know,' I say, laughing.

'I'm serious,' she says.

'I know you are and I am too.'

We hug each other tight and when we separate I say, 'I thought you were gonna squeeze me to death there. You're stronger than you look, bitch.'

'You don't know this, but I'm actually Superwoman,' she says.

'I already knew that. I was just waiting for you to catch up.'

There's tears in her eyes. And mine. Can't lie.

Becks goes aw and snaps some pictures and then takes a couple of selfies with us posing like pop stars.

Lauryn says, 'I've got a name for the baby. I'm gonna call him Jack. After his auntie.'

I literally shriek and we end up hugging and kissing again.

'It's a good name,' Becks says. 'Suits him. He's going to be strong like his auntie.'

Becks rocks the baby gently and her face is all soft. She smells the top of his head and plants a little kiss on the end of his nose. You'd almost think she was the mum.

'Come on, babes,' I say. 'We gotta move.'

Becks gives the baby to Lauryn.

'Laters, baby Jack,' I say. 'Love you.'

Then I'm outta there. I'm feeling very emotional.

Walking down the street holding my hand, Becks says, 'Lauryn told me all about Jimmy the Indian.'

Over a couple of glasses of wine I tell her about how Jimmy and my dad were friends. And how Jimmy might be even friendlier with my mum, though it's not something I like to think about. And then I tell her all the shit about growing up and Mum not being around and me and Lauryn on our own and all that shit. I didn't mean to start talking about this cos I was happy and them days back when I was growing up it was not a happy time. But Becks is a serious girl. She likes to party and she's a lot of fun, but deep down Becks is serious. Sometimes when she's fed up of work she talks about retraining as a psychotherapist. She's deep. And she cares about other people. About what traumas they've had and how they can get fixed. So the talk is serious. About family and about my dad and how he's living in Toronto now and how I feel about him. Becks talks about her dad, who she don't get on with.

'He's a cold man,' she says. 'He never shows affection. I don't understand how he can be so detached from his children. I don't understand how you can have a child and not love it. When I have a child, that child is going to be so loved by me.'

'And by me,' I say.

She looks at me like what do I mean?

'Maybe I'm assuming too much,' I say. 'But if you have a child, I want to be part of that.'

'You do?'

'Course,' I say. 'I ain't letting you get away.'

There's literally tears in her eyes. And mine. The waiter sees us and a couple of minutes later brings us two more drinks.

'On the house,' he says.

'Bless,' I say. 'Thank you.'

'People are good,' Becks says when he's gone. 'They're just good.'

That's Becks all over. She's just very caring.

I tell her about the yoga class and how naughty Lauryn was and we start laughing like idiots.

We're still laughing when we get home. It ain't that late, not even eleven and we're joking about this nice-looking girl we saw in the wine bar.

'You're a proper criss baddie, you know,' I tell her. 'I am so lucky.'

'You are very lucky,' she says and kisses me.

'Do you even love me?' I say, just being silly and a little drunk.

'You know I love you,' she says. 'She was nice-looking though.'

'You're out of order,' I say. 'You're not even her type anyway. I'm more her type.'

Becks just laughs. It's a beautiful laugh, a little bit naughty and posh. 'Yeah, yeah, yeah. That's what you'd like to think.'

I can hear the baby crying upstairs.

'Let me go check on Lauryn and the baby,' I say, starting up the stairs.

Becks is getting a bottle of wine. 'Do you want one?'

'Yeah, go on.'

I find the baby in his cot in Lauryn's bedroom. He's crying hard, very upset. 'All right, little man,' I say, trying to soothe him. 'What's happening, what's happening? Let's find Mummy.'

I cross to the bathroom. I'm already putting together in

my head the very harsh talk I'm gonna give Lauryn for leaving the baby crying like this. 'Lauryn?'

Lauryn's in the bath. I can see straight off she's dead. Her face isn't completely under the water. But it's just the look of her. I know it. She's dead. I pull her up outta the water and shout for Becks. The baby is still crying his eyes out.

I'm holding Lauryn in my arms. 'Wake up, wake up,' I tell her. Like what a mad thing to say cos I already knew she ain't gonna wake up. I keep calling her name like she's gonna come back. But that ain't happening. I'm crying and calling for Becks and telling Lauryn to come back, over and over.

Becks comes running in. 'What is it?' The look on her face when she sees me kneeling at the bath with Lauryn in my arms.

'You need to call someone,' I wail.

How many times do you have to say someone's name before they come back? Maybe that's why when you're with someone you love and they've passed you keep saying their name, over and over. Because maybe there's a magic number and if you get to that number they'll open their eyes and look at you and smile and tell you they're back and that they love you.

But then I see the wrap next to the candle beside the bath and I know exactly what's happened and I know there ain't no magic number and no matter how many times I call her name, Lauryn is never, ever coming back.

I don't remember too good everything that happened next. I remember pulling Lauryn out of the water. Becks was helping me. We got Lauryn on the floor. And I remember kneeling over her and crying buckets.

Later, Becks told me that I just kept saying to Lauryn, 'Come back, come back.'

I don't know if I did say that. If I did, it was a dumb thing to say. Nobody comes back from where Lauryn was. It didn't make no difference what I said.

Lauryn was gone and she wasn't coming back.

THE LIMP

Ask me what time it is. I don't know.

Ask me what day it is. I don't know.

Ask me what year it is. I don't know.

I don't know if it's day or night. I don't know if the sky is blue. I don't know what colour the leaves on the trees are. I don't know left from right. I don't know up from down. I don't know anything. I'm numb. I'm in a heap on the sofa crying.

If it wasn't for Becks, I wouldn't know what to do. Becks makes the calls. The ambulance comes. The paramedics make some calls. Then the feds come.

Other people come but I don't know who they are. They go in and out. They're rude. Going in rooms, looking at my shit, lifting stuff up and seeing if there's more to it. There ain't. Cos I ain't dumb enough to keep anything in my house. That's just basic. If you're on the road, you don't keep straps or food in your yard. I ain't worried about them finding anything. Turns out they're forensics and the police photographer.

The ambulance takes Lauryn away and the feds stay

and ask their questions. Even though I'm crying and can't see straight, I know the feds are suspicious. They're thinking three Black girls, heroin, nice house, nice car, what's going on here?

I don't remember the exact details of what they ask but I can't tell them much even if I wanted, which I don't. I mean, I genuinely can't cos I didn't know Lauryn was using. Yeah, I found the wrap – I don't tell the feds about that, of course – but Lauryn swore blind to me she wouldn't do it again and after our sisters' day out I believed her. It was like she said, she just wanted to take the edge off. I didn't know she was just waiting for me and Becks to leave the house so she could get in the bath and get high.

But the feds keep prodding away. Did I know Lauryn was using? Do I know where she got the drugs? Did I give her the drugs? I told them no. No, I fucking did not give her the drugs.

It helps that I ain't got a criminal record. Not even for shoplifting, and I did plenty of that when I was at school. So when they ask me my full name and date of birth and they check me out I know I don't have nothing to worry about. They ask me what I do for work and about my house and my car. It's all legit. Lithe, Dushane's bookkeeper who he inherited from Lizzie, made sure everything was accounted for. Lithe sat me down one day and said, 'Jaq, you're earning a lot of money. You need to be able to account for it because no matter how careful you are one day you will have to answer questions about how you can afford to have such a beautiful house and such a nice car.'

It cost me Ps cos Lithe don't come cheap. But she set it all up so if anyone ever asked I could tell them I was employed by some bullshit company she set up.

Lithe warned me this day would come. I just never thought it would be the day my sister died in the bath.

It also helps that Becks' dad is a big legit businessman with contacts in high places. He knows all the right people. Politicians, entrepreneurs, people in sports and television and newspapers. I hadn't met him before cos it's tricky between him and Becks, but he came over when Becks told him what had happened. His name's Robert and he carries himself like someone with money who's used to getting his own way, which intimidates the fuck outta the feds. So they can't question me that deep.

I don't remember going to bed that night or the next one. I'm not even sure I went to bed the night after that. The next few days went by in a blur. Every time I used the bathroom I looked at the bath and I had to close my eyes. Delivery drivers came with flowers. We had so many that we didn't have enough things to put them in. The feds came again. Same old bullshit. The funeral director also came, talking about arrangements and options. There were also a whole load of forms to go through and sign. I was in my own trance. The forms didn't mean anything to me.

Becks takes care of it all. That girl, she's so fucking impressive and she's with me the whole time. She's taking care of the baby, dealing with all the paperwork you gotta deal with when someone's died. She's talking to the funeral parlour about whether we want a burial or cremation and when we want it to be. I don't know, I say. It can't be too soon cos my dad will want to come over from Canada. Becks relays it all to the funeral people. She's just as exhausted as I am but she's holding it all together. It just makes me cry thinking about her and how much she loves me.

Then a social worker comes to check on baby Jack,

asking about how he ain't even had his name registered, saying how they might have to take him into care. I tell her there ain't no way that's happening. She says they'll have to review the case.

'His name's Jack,' I say. 'You review the case when you want. But now, get the fuck outta my fucking house.'

Becks sees her out and I can hear her at the door trying to calm the situation down, saying, 'Jaqueline has had a terrible shock. She was very close with her sister.'

That might of been the first time I cracked a smile since Lauryn died.

Jaqueline.

No one's called me Jaqueline since the teachers at school. Becks is pretty smooth. I suppose it comes from her marketing job. In marketing they all talk that bullshit, not that I know anything about it.

I never look at my phones. Becks goes through the missed calls and messages as she's giving baby Jack his bottle.

'Kieron says when can I see you, bruv? Kiss, kiss, kiss. What should I say?' she asks.

'Not now.'

'Sure? Might do you good to see him. He's a good friend. I like Kieron.'

'I said not now.'

She types it into the phone and sends.

'Romy wants to see you as well?'

'Nah. Anything from Sully?'

Becks shakes her head.

'Check the other phone,' I tell her.

'I've already looked,' she says. 'There's nothing from him. There's three missed calls and nine messages from Sharon.'

I snatch the phone and look at the messages. They're all the same thing. Call me. Where are you? Need to talk. Urgent.

'What's that about?' Becks asks.

'Nothing,' I say.

I met Sharon through Becks so a friend of hers is calling and texting her girlfriend. Obvious she's gonna raise an eyebrow. Fuck knows what's she thinking.

'There's nothing going on with Sharon,' I say. 'You know that, right?'

'Right,' she says, but there's a little bit of reservation in her tone.

The doorbell goes.

'I don't wanna see no one,' I tell Becks as she gets the door.

Then who comes in? Fucking Mandy. She's carrying all these bags of food.

'Thank you so much, Mandy,' Becks says, being all marketing, all polite. She don't like offending people. 'But Jaq really wants just to be on her own.'

'I'm not staying,' Mandy says, bustling into the kitchen with her bags. 'I just brought some food.'

She hoists the bags onto the kitchen counter and looks over at me on the sofa under the blanket.

'Are you eating, Jaq?' Mandy says.

'Yes,' I say in a harsh way. Impatient. I don't wanna talk about eating.

She takes out a container. 'I made some ackee and saltfish for you.'

'Thank you,' Becks says. 'That's so kind.'

Mandy is just busting to get talking. I can see it. I look away.

Then I hear Becks say, 'Would you like a cup of tea?'

No! What the fuck is that girl thinking? And before I know it Mandy is drinking one of Becks' herbal fucking infusions.

'Try to get her to eat,' Mandy says to Becks. 'Even if it's just a little.'

'I'm fucking here, you know,' I spit out. 'Don't talk about me like I'm some idiot.'

'I hope you got my flowers,' Mandy says.

Becks nods. 'They were lovely.'

Lying bitch. We got so many we could of opened our own flower shop. Becks can't remember which ones were the ones Mandy sent.

Mandy looks over at me. She says slowly, 'Was Lauryn talking to anyone about it?'

'What?' I say. 'Lauryn weren't some fucking dirty nittie. She'd just had her kid. She was stressed. She needed to take the edge off.'

'I knew a lotta girls in the pen that got hooked on that shit, same ting. Saying they was just taking the edge off and then it just spirals.'

'It didn't spiral. I told you she weren't no fucking nittie. She didn't OD.'

'Where was she getting it, you reckon?'

'What's that supposed to mean? What are you saying?'

'It's a question, Jaq. That's all.'

'Well, what's with all the fucking questions?'

'She's just asking, Jaq,' Becks says. 'I mean, I asked the same thing.'

'Just trying to make it make sense,' Mandy says.

'It ain't hard to understand. She drowned cos she couldn't handle that shit. She weren't about that life.'

Becks says, 'Mandy's not saying she was.'

Mandy has the sense to know when she should leave. She smiles and thanks Becks for the tea and says she has to be going. She digs around in her bag and says like she's only just thought of it, 'Oh yeah, I brung you these.'

She passes me two books. They both have pictures of women on the front. The first is a Black woman with a big afro in a black tee and short black skirt resting her chin on her hand. The cover says *Angela Y. Davis* at the top and *An Autobiography* at the bottom. She looks like a queen. The second is a white woman with a side parting and she has her hand up on her face as well.

'That's Bernadette Devlin,' Mandy says. 'That's her autobiography, *The Price of My Soul*. She's Irish. The Black sister is Angela Davis. She's a legend.'

I look at Mandy like what the fuck?

'My sister has died and you're giving me fucking books?' I shout at her. 'Normal people bring fucking flowers. I don't care about your political shit.'

'What we did that day for Kieron, that was political.'

'Nah,' I say. 'Kieron's my guy. That's why I done it.'

'You remind me of both of them,' Mandy says, 'Bernadette and Angela. You got that power that they have. Inside. Deep inside.'

I literally throw the books back at her. Mandy catches one and Becks picks the other one off the floor and hands it to her, kind of embarrassed.

'I just wanna see the girl who was with me the day we forced the feds and Immigration to let Kieron go. And all the idiots could do was drive off with an empty van,' Mandy says.

I don't wanna talk to her no more.

Mandy starts talking about being in the pen, about how a man died who shouldn't have died and how she was fully involved. I already know the story and I'm only half listening cos I got my own problems. My sister is dead. But Mandy goes on about how the first few years she never accepted responsibility and that's when I know she ain't talking about herself, she's talking about me.

'What are you trying to say here?' I ask her.

'Jaq, I'm gonna say it clear cos it needs to be said. Beautiful Lauryn's dead cos she took drugs that you sell.'

I've heard enough. I smack her in the face.

'Get out!'

'Slapping me ain't gonna change that,' she says.

'Get the fuck outta my yard.'

'It's too late for Lauryn,' she says, 'but it ain't too late for her baby.'

She turns and goes and I'm glad to see her gone. I never liked the bitch in the first place. But there was something she said. She asked where Lauryn got the drugs.

I start thinking about who served up Lauryn. Not for the first time. Whoever it was, they're gonna have a serious problem. I'll find them. Whoever they are. I'm thinking about what I'm gonna say to them, do to them, when I hear voices. Mandy talking to someone who's obviously just arriving.

'I'm good,' she says. 'What you saying?'

'Just here to see Jaq, innit.'

It's Sully. Fuck me.

'Are you serious?' I hear Mandy say. 'You know what happened, innit?'

'Yeah. It's terrible, I can't lie,' Sully says.

'Yeah, heroin is pretty fucking terrible, ain't it,' Mandy says. 'I mean, would you take it?'

'What?'

'That's a no, right?' Mandy says.

'What are you on about?' Sully says.

'So you don't take it, I'm assuming. Dushane don't take it. Dris didn't take it. None of them man that work for you take it. Why not? Cos you know what it does to people. But you'll sell it to anyone stupid or desperate enough to buy it. Even though you know you're selling them poison.'

'Feel better? Now you got that off your chest?' Sully says.

'You think I'm done?'

'You better be cos I'm here to see my friend.'

When I hear Sully call me his friend I feel something inside, I can't lie. Sully doesn't call people his friend who he doesn't rate highly.

I hear Mandy going on, 'People die because of you, Sully. All for your pockets.'

I don't hear Sully saying anything but I can imagine him staring at Mandy with those big eyes of his, letting her know that now's the time to back off, if she has any sense.

'I'm just here to see my friend,' he says at last.

And a couple of seconds later he appears in front of me.

'How you doing?' he says.

I just shrug. How do you answer that question? Becks closes the door and comes back inside with baby Jack.

'This the likkle man?'

Sully leans over to look at the baby.

'He's as good as gold,' Becks says.

Sully turns to me and says, 'Just wanted to make sure you're awright. Are you? Awright?'

'Fucked if I know.'

'I know that feeling.'

Sully sits down slowly. When I think about it, Sully does everything slow. I don't mean like old man slow. Just everything very deliberate. I mean everything. I don't think I've ever seen him run. He rubs his eyes and fixes me with a look.

'All that shit going round in your head will haunt you. Cos you loved Lauryn. That's your sis. But this ain't on you, Jaq. You know that, right?'

'Yeah, I know.'

'People will tell you that it passes. Someone told me that once. It'll pass. But it don't. It don't ever go away.'

I know he's thinking about Jason here. Jason got torched when them racists down in Ramsgate firebombed the house Sully was using when he got outta jail and him and Jason went to do some business down there at the seaside.

So I say, 'Jason ain't never gone away?'

'Nah,' he says slowly and he raises his right hand to his nostrils. 'Sometimes I think I can still smell the smoke from the fire on my hands. You smell anything?'

He holds his hands out for me to sniff.

'No,' I tell him.

'Sometimes in the middle of the night the smell is so strong it wakes me up.'

'But it ain't there. There ain't no smell.'

'There is. But you weren't there so you can't smell it. Losing someone is like being in a car crash. You survive but you walk away with a limp. You're gonna have that limp for the rest of your life. There ain't no way round that. But there's limps and there's limps and there's work you can do to make that limp as small as possible, so it's hardly noticeable.'

There's the difference between Sully and Dushane right there. Dushane ain't sent no message or flowers. But even if he comes round to see me he would never be able to talk like Sully. Dushane's lost people close to him. His mum. His cousin in Jamaica. But Dushane ain't got no limp.

'Swear down,' Sully says. 'If there's anything you need. You've been there for me. I'm here for you. Always will be.'

He gets up to go.

'Actually there is something.'

'Talk to me.'

'I wanna name. I wanna know who served up Lauryn.'

Sully takes a breath. He would of known this was coming. 'I said this ain't on you. And it ain't. And it ain't on whoever sold to Lauryn neither.'

'I want a name.'

'I can't do that.'

'You said you were here for me.'

'That's why I can't give you a name.' He looks around the flat. 'You've got something good here. Don't make the limp no bigger than what it has to be.'

'Nice to meet you,' he says to Becks and then he's gone.

CANDIDATES

Ask me what time it is. I still don't know.

Ask me what day it is. I might be able to tell you.

Ask me what year it is. I definitely know what year we're in.

I know the sky is blue, but sometimes I'm still not sure if it's day or night.

As for up and down, I still have no idea what's the right way up. About anything.

The numbness is starting to wear off, but I don't feel normal. I feel angry. I wanna know who served up Lauryn and no one is telling me, and that makes me more angry.

I'm not the only one who's angry. Sharon is texting me all the time. Sharon is very angry. Where am I? Why am I not replying to her? Can she rely on me? Time is running out. How I need to call her asap. I don't like her cop tone so I don't even think about replying.

One afternoon of whatever day it was Becks is on her Zooms and shit and I'm giving baby Jack his bottle when the door goes. I'm thinking it's gonna be Sharon. Being a fed, she could easily find my address.

But it ain't Sharon. It's Jimmy the Indian.

Jimmy steps inside and he gives me a kiss on the cheek. He's all dressed up in his snazzy three-piece suit and a shirt as bright white as his teeth. There are gold rings on just about every finger and he's wearing a Rolex. I ain't a tall girl and Jimmy's not much taller than me. But sideways he is twice my size at least. It's not fat. It's muscle. Jimmy is a solid block of concrete. I can feel the muscle as he's hugging me. He makes a big fuss about baby Jack, saying how beautiful he is, just like his mum. He's got flowers, he's got a Harrods Food Hall bag and he has a bottle of white rum. I ain't interested in the flowers or the food but I get two glasses and we sit on the sofa and start on the bottle.

Jimmy flashes his white teeth and says, 'It was your mum who told me about Lauryn. She's devastated.'

'If she's devastated, why hasn't she come to see me?'

'I told her not to come. She's really taken it badly and she's all over the place and having her here wouldn't do you any good, trust me.'

Maybe Jimmy and Mum are together? Who knows? Well, I really want to know so I ask, 'How often do you see my mum?' I don't manage to make the question sound quite as casual as I want it to.

Jimmy takes a sip of his rum and says slowly, 'It's probably time you should know, Jaq. Violet and I have become quite close.'

Violet and I? Quite close?

'Are you two together?'

'Well, together I don't know. Your mum is a complicated woman.'

'Tell me about it.'

'Violet has a lot of demons. I don't kid myself. Your dad is the love of her life. I'm just standing in until Vincent comes back.'

'You seriously think Dad is coming back?'

He sucks in a lotta air through his teeth and breathes out slow. 'No, I don't, to be honest. But what I think is beside the point. Violet is convinced he'll come back to her someday. I can't tell her that it's not going to happen because she'd think I was just being manipulative or jealous or possessive. Which could be partly true, who knows. But anyway, she's truly devastated about Lauryn.'

'Does Dad know?'

'Vincent's changed his number. Your dad does that quite a lot. When a man changes his number as often as your dad does it's not usually a sign that things are going well for him. He either owes money or someone's after him, either the police or a woman or a gangster. But I'm sure I can find a way to get him a message if you want that.'

I think about it for a moment and then I say, 'Yeah, I think he should know his daughter's passed. I hope he'll come to the funeral.'

'Leave it with me. I'll get a message to him.'

'And maybe you could tell him, you know, that if he wants to get in touch with me, he can.'

'I'll tell him that,' he says. He pats my arm. 'How are you holding up?'

I tell Jimmy the whole story starting with the wrap I found and the sisters' day out we had when we bumped into him, and going to Shelley's and getting our nails done, and then the bath.

He asks about the babyfather and I tell him – without naming names – that the babyfather was a controlling and abusive bastard and that he ain't around no more and isn't ever going to be.

Jimmy understands what I'm saying, but being the professional he is, he don't comment on it. There ain't even a sideways look. He understands.

Jimmy pours out more rum. He says how nice the yard is and asks if it's mine and that takes us into the criminal side of things. Jimmy knows all about the proceeds of crime and that shit.

'The Crown Prosecution Service has this specialist unit called CPSPOC,' he says. 'It does asset recovery and they work with the HMRC and social security to target anyone they think is making money from crime. Well, I say anyone. Obviously, they don't go after the real crooks, the billionaires and the oligarchs and politicians. But they do go after the likes of you and me, so I hope you've a good story for them and all the right paperwork if they ever come knocking.'

I tell him about Lithe and how she's set it all up for me with all the correct paperwork and invoices and shit. He says he likes the sound of this Lithe.

'The problem with most criminals,' he says, 'is they think just because they make a couple of mil on the road they can spend a couple of mil. They can't. They have to spend half of it getting things straight so they can spend the other half. It's still a lot of money. I'm glad to hear you're being smart. I didn't expect anything less.'

After his feed, baby Jack needs changed. Jimmy does it for me and he does it so quick and expert I'm wondering how many kids he's got. I never asked him before.

'I have six,' he says.

I ask him about them.

'They're all good,' he says with a big smile. 'Well, apart

from Alfie. Alfie was a bit of a hothead. He got killed in a knife fight in 2011. But the others are all doing well. Every single one of them except Alfie went to university. Adam got a PhD in quantum physics. He's in Amsterdam with his girlfriend Ana. They have a start-up and it seems to be going very well from what they tell me, although to be honest I have no idea what a start-up is. Annie's still at Oxford doing her PhD. Ollie got married to a lovely Canadian girl Em. They're living in Toronto, doing very well. I was out visiting them when I bumped into Vincent in the restaurant like I told you.'

When Jimmy talks about his kids, he's just so proud of them. It's kind of sweet. He apologises, 'Sorry, I'm boasting. But that's what parents do. They boast about their kids.'

'Mine never did.'

'Violet always tells me how smart you are, how quick. What a great girl.'

I don't believe him. I pour the drinks this time. I wanna get back to talking about criminal things.

'You know one thing you told me years ago?' I say. 'You said that when a chess player is looking at the position on the board for a move he doesn't just make the move when he thinks he's found it. He goes through the other possibilities first, the candidates.'

'Candidates, well done,' he says. 'Well remembered.'

'The thing is, I have this situation, and I'm trying to go through the candidates so I can find the right move. And to be honest, after what happened Lauryn, I don't even know if I wanna do it no more. I can't make my mind up. I can't think straight.'

'That's normal,' he says. 'Do you want to tell me what this particular situation involves?'

Do I tell him or not? The thing with Jimmy is he's got a wise head. And that time he was nicked for the bank robbery all them years ago, he never gave a single name, even though he would of got some years off his sentence. I heard Dad say more than once that Jimmy was staunch. That was the word the old gangster generation used about someone you could totally trust. Staunch. Jimmy never talked out of turn.

I swear him to secrecy and then tell him about Sharon and the Dickie Simms stash. Jimmy listens carefully, twisting his rings one by one. He has this habit when he's listening of twisting the ring on the little finger of his left hand and then working all the way across to the little finger of his right hand. That's when you know you've got his attention and he's concentrating.

'What are your candidates?' Jimmy asks when I finish.

'Well,' I say, 'first is I don't do it. But then I miss out on the chance of a lifetime and money that's gonna change my life.'

'All right,' he says. 'That's candidate one.'

'Second, I do it and I do it alone, which means I get to keep more of the Ps for myself.'

'Do you think you can handle it alone?'

'I don't know yet. I don't know what kind of opps there's gonna be.'

'OK. It's a candidate move worth considering even if you discard it later. But as you're aware, it could be very risky without the right backup. You could end up dead or in jail with no money at all.'

'Or I could end up with a lot of money,' I say.

'You could. Any other candidates?'

'So, third, I do it with my guy Kieron. But Kieron is

having problems with Immigration. Also, his mum is very sick with cancer and I don't know where his head is right now.'

'I read all about that thing on Summerhouse with you and Mandy. Great photo of the two of you.'

'Thanks,' I say. 'Fourth, if Kieron won't do it, I get someone else to do it with me.'

'Got anyone in mind?'

'Yeah, I got someone in mind,' I say.

'It has to be someone you can trust.'

'I trust this person a hundred per cent.'

'That's a lot of per cent,' Jimmy says, twisting his rings. 'Do you want to tell me who it is?'

I take a big swallow of the rum. It burns my throat on the way down but once it's in my belly it feels nice and warm.

'It's you, Jimmy,' I say.

Jimmy leans back into the sofa. I don't think he was expecting that. He doesn't say anything for a long time.

'What do you say?' I ask him.

'Tell me about the cozzer, this Sharon woman.'

'I met her through my girlfriend Becks. All I know is she likes to party. She likes her drugs and she wants the money.'

'You said she has this colleague with the snitch who's been planning this with her?'

'Yeah, but I ain't met him or the snitch. Only her. I don't know who he is.'

'Do you think she's told anyone else?'

'I don't think so cos she's very nervous about this. She gave me this burner phone so there's nothing on our real phones.'

'Sounds like she's being careful at least. How much does she want?'

'She asked for half the value, which she says is between five and seven mil.'

'The police have no idea about the street value of drugs. They make the numbers high so it makes them look good. But even if she's exaggerating, it's probably worth a tidy sum.'

Jimmy turns to baby Jack and makes baby noises. I'm disappointed cos I can already see Jimmy's backing out of this. Maybe I should go back and try Kieron again? Or maybe I should talk to Romy?

Jimmy takes a long drink of rum. He says, 'I'll be honest with you, Jaq. Looking at these candidates, the best move you can make . . . if you want my advice . . .'

'That's why I'm asking.'

'All right, but I don't think you'll like it.'

'Go on.'

'My advice is don't do it. Don't do it solo, don't do it with Kieron, don't do it with anyone else. Don't do it.'

'Why?'

'I told you you wouldn't like it.'

'This is life-changing money we're talking about, Jimmy.'

Jimmy pours two more drinks. Big ones. He doesn't smile. He looks very serious.

He says, 'The problem here is that you're working with police. You'd think old bill would make good criminals. After all, they get to see all our mistakes, don't they? And we make a lot of mistakes. They see where we go wrong, all the hundreds of ways we fuck up. Pardon my French.'

'I didn't know fuck was French, innit,' I say.

Jimmy flashes a dazzling white smile. 'But even though

old bill see all our mistakes, when they turn to crime, as more and more of them are doing every day, they never seem to learn. They still make really basic mistakes.'

'Sharon's being really careful,' I remind him.

'Them fucking up isn't even the worst of working with crooked police. The worst is that when they do something illegal, they feel guilty. They can't help it. They're like Catholics. Guilt is ingrained. So when they get the tap on the shoulder, they start blubbing and spill their guts faster than cute little baby Jack here falls asleep after his feed. They'll confess absolutely everything and they'll give up every name they can think of, including their own mother's. But your name will be the first on their list.'

I'm definitely disappointed now.

'Thank you for the offer,' he says. 'But if old bill are involved, my advice is walk away. If you don't, you'll be walking right into a big mess.'

We drink another glass and then Jimmy goes. I can't decide what I want to do. How long is it gonna be before I can see straight again?

SOMETHING I NEED TO TAKE CARE OF

The night after Jimmy comes to see me, I dream about Lauryn. It ain't a nice dream. Lauryn is on the floor in her bedroom at my mum's house and I'm punching her over and over and calling her a stupid fucking selfish stupid bitch. Lauryn looks up at me with big, frightened eyes and just keeps saying, 'Jackie, please don't.' But I keep hitting her and hitting her and she just keeps looking up at me with this sad, hurt, frightened look. She begs me to stop. But I don't. I keep hitting her.

All of this is real. I mean it happened in real life after Lauryn almost got Sully killed with her loose pillow talk when he was going to Jason's cremation that time. I had to beg Dushane for her life, innit, and then I lost it with Lauryn. I fully admit it. I can still see the way Lauryn looked up at me. The fear. I hate what I did then. I hate it. But that wasn't the worst of what I do in the dream. In the dream, after I stop beating her, she holds out her open hand to me like she's asking for help. I don't take her hand. What I do is I drop a wrap of dark in her palm and close her fingers around it. Lauryn takes the wrap and goes and gets in the bath and that's all I remember.

When I wake up, I can't shake the dream. I run a finger over my knuckles like I can still feel them swollen after beating on Lauryn. And then, don't ask me why, I hold my hand out, open, the palm up, like Lauryn did, and I'm staring at my hand and Becks looks at me and says, 'Babes, are you OK?'

I just stare at my hand.

'Babes,' she says, and she puts her arms around me.

'I killed Lauryn,' I say.

'What are you talking about?' Becks says, pulling me in close to her. 'Of course you didn't.'

'I did,' I say. 'I killed her.'

I killed her with my drugs. Or Sully's drugs, I suppose. But it's the same thing, innit.

Becks tries to calm me down, but I get out of bed. I don't need support now, or love. I just need to think things through, by myself. Then I see bare messages from Sharon on the burner she gave me. She's upped her tone. Saying about how I've let her down so bad. How I've ruined everything. How I promised I would do it and now I've just disappeared. How she trusted me and what a mistake that was.

And there's this final message, which I really don't care for. Real Sharon cop tone now, the kind I really don't like. She says: if I was a different kind of person I could make things very difficult for you. Don't make me be that kind of person. Answer my fucking messages.

Jimmy warned me. If a crooked fed's involved, walk away. Otherwise you're walking into a big mess. I look at Sharon's messages again. I feel like I'm running out of road. I don't see what my options are.

I go in Lauryn's room. Baby Jack is in his cot so I chat shit to him just to get my mind off this shit.

'We might have to call you Delroy, you know? For real,' I say to him. 'Me and your mum was cracking up over that, do you remember? Nooo, you're trying to tell me, not Delroy, anything but Delroy. I can see it in your eyes. Definitely got Mummy's beautiful eyes.'

I put my finger out and his little fingers curl around it. Baby Jack gazes at me and I stare back at him. I start to calm down a little. I lean in and kiss his forehead.

'You know what would be a perfect name for him?' Becks says, coming in.

'We've got a name for him. Jack. After me.'

'We could call him after his mum.'

'Lauryn's a girl's name.'

'Laurence,' Becks says.

'So what you're saying is he would be Laurence Lawrence?'

Becks laughs.

'You do know my second name is Lawrence, don't you?'

Laurence Lawrence. It's mad. I bust out laughing.

'That's so nice,' Becks says. 'Seeing you laugh again.'

The doorbell goes. Becks sighs and goes to get it and I get back to the baby.

'So listen, baby Jack. Do you want to be Jack or Laurence or Delroy? Jack, right? Yeah, you do. You're definitely Jack.'

Becks comes back in with Kieron.

'Thought you was in Rwanda, bruv,' I say.

'Nah, man,' Kieron says. 'Got you to thank for that, innit.'

'Not me. It was Mandy, weren't it.'

'Yeah, well. Sorry to drop in like this. Man's devastated about Lauryn, innit.'

'It's bless.'

'But I need to chat to you.'

I can see Becks is not impressed.

'Go on,' I say.

'We've got a problem. Fields lot had a madness on their spot this morning. The place is covered with feds.'

'Seriously?' Becks says. 'You think this is the right time to be talking about this?'

'Allow it, babe,' I tell her.

'You don't need to hear this,' she says.

'I do,' I tell her. I say it a bit harsh and Becks looks away. 'What happened?' I ask Kieron.

'Them lot brought some personal beef shit to the spot, I don't know. Got their food taken. One of the youngers got nicked. One of the opps is in hospital.'

'Look, Kieron,' Becks interrupts. 'I really don't think, at this time, after what's happened, that this is appropriate.'

'I said it's calm,' I say.

'I can deal with it,' Kieron says. 'I just need you to tell me what you want done.'

'Nah, come, we go,' I say, getting to my feet.

'It's good, seriously. I can handle this.'

'Can I just ask?' Becks says. 'If you can handle it, why did you come here?'

'She's my boss. I had to,' Kieron says.

'I need to get out of this place for a bit. Come on.'

'Jaq, are you for real? Think about this.'

'There's something I need to take care of.'

I do need to take care of something, but I also need to get out of the house, can't lie.

'Yes, there is. He's right there,' Becks says, nodding to the baby.

I ignore her and leave with Kieron. We go in his car, heading to the Fields, to Si's yard. On the way, I ask him what he's hearing about the Irish problem.

'Sully brought this fella Jonny to the bando,' he says.

'Irish Jonny?'

'Yeah.'

'He brought man to the bando? What the fuck?'

I'm a bit confused. Cos you don't bring someone to the place you've got your food, where you're operating out of, unless you trust them. I mean, the bando's secret. So what does it mean if Sully brought Jonny to the bando?

'Sully ain't talking to me about it,' Kieron goes on. 'But from what I can see, Sully ain't got a lotta options. The Irish robbed the food and they control the links out in Spain and Morocco.'

'Sully ain't gonna let it run that way for long,' I say.

'I don't know, Jaq. Them Irish have a lotta army. I don't see there's much Sully can do.'

'My money's on Sully,' I say.

'I hope so,' Kieron says, 'cos, bruv, if the Irish take over, what happens to you and me?'

I've been thinking the same thing. Kieron asks about the Sharon thing. I tell him how she's getting narky and what Jimmy said about working with crooked cops.

'That mean you don't wanna do it no more?' he asks.

'I don't know,' I say. 'Maybe. Depends.'

'On what?'

'I don't know anything any more, bruv,' I say. 'Let's see how it rolls.'

'Cool.'

I can hear music blasting inside when I knock Si's door. One of the Fields youngers, Tyrone, lets us in. I march right in the living room where Si is stretched out on this big sofa with three of four of the Fields lot.

Si is this tall, thin guy with a shaved head. His face is just eyes and bones. He can look very scary, but I don't rate him. Jamie, when he ran the Fields mob, didn't look hard. But he was hard. Jamie was a stone-cold killer and he was intelligent. Now Si is running what's left of the Fields and he ain't a killer and he ain't that intelligent neither.

They've been smoking weed and drinking and are pretty chilled. But when they see me the atmosphere changes.

'Turn that shit off,' I say.

Tyrone turns the music off. That's when I see Stefan on the sofa next to Si. The youth stares at me, probably remembering that time I talked to him and his brother at Mandy's. He said he never saw the so-called mysterious figure who shot Jamie, but of course he saw. He obviously ain't told the feds or I would of been pulled in. But, I mean, what would you do if someone killed your brother? I know what I would do. I would go after that person. I wouldn't say nothing. I wouldn't make no threats. I would wait. Everybody soon or later lets their guard down. That's what I would wait for. I'd walk up to them when they ain't thinking they have to be careful, when their mind is wandering, when they're thinking about that pair of trainers they wanna buy, or about that girl they wanna ask to go for a drink. Then BANG! Shoot him in the head.

Looking at Stef, I know that's what's in his head. I can see it. I know he's waiting for the right time. Sully's gonna have to watch himself. But he knows that. And knowing Sully, he's thinking about taking steps with Stef, just to be on the safe side.

I look round the room. 'Well, this is a fucking mess, innit,' I say.

'We'll sort it,' Si says.

'I know that, bruv. Course you're gonna sort it. You lost us P today. A whole brick's worth.'

'We're rolling out,' a girl I don't know says. 'We're gonna find it.'

'Are you dumb?' I say. 'You ain't gonna find no food that's been robbed. Them man have boyed you off and that's that. What? Are you gonna drive round and waste another day's earning? You know what, I don't even want you lot retaliating. You got one of them man in A&E, so now focus on making the Ps back, innit. Put up your prices, hustle harder. Do you understand what I'm saying to you? Shit's fucking amateur.'

'We can't let these man violate us like that,' Tyrone says.

'But you already did, though,' I say. 'And that's why you're gonna be too busy making back what you fucking lost to be running up on anyone. You got that?'

The room goes silent. They're all staring at me.

'Is that gonna be a problem?' I ask.

'No problems here,' Si says.

Jamie would never have said that. I didn't like man, but Jamie was a leader. That's how far the Fields have fallen. You know things are bad when someone like Si's your boss.

'Only solutions, yeah?' I say.

'Yeah,' Si says.

'Say less. In a bit, yeah?' I nudge Kieron to leave.

'Shit's amateur cos you man are dunning all our soldiers,' Tyrone says to my back as I'm heading to the door.

I stop and turn on him. 'What? Go on. Speak up. Say what you're fucking saying, big man.'

'How are we meant to be running this ting if you keep dunning the mandem?' Tyrone says.

'Are you mad?'

'Am I mad? Maybe I missed something? Maybe Jamie's still alive? Maybe Kit's still breathing?'

'Sit the fuck down,' I tell him.

'I'm just asking the question.'

I push Tyrone into a chair. 'I said sit the fuck down.'

There's some stirrings, like they wanna have a pop at me.

'Yo, yo, yo,' Kieron says. 'You gotta chill, man. It's not that.'

They settle down again.

'No one knows who done Jamie,' I say, looking right at Stef on the sofa beside Si. He don't contradict me. I go on, 'Man was a hard fucking worker and he was the only one you fucking little dickheads listened to so why the fuck would we want him in the ground?'

Stef is staring at me. He knows I'm chatting shit. But he also knows he has to keep his mouth shut.

'So I suppose you don't know what happened to Kit?' the girl asks, snide like.

I look at Kieron. He nods like he's saying, go ahead, tell them. I kind of laugh cos I'm gonna enjoy this part. I look them over, one by one, and I say, 'The person that done Kit was Jamie.'

They really don't like hearing the truth. Si gets to his

feet for the first time, like he's had enough. Stef stares at me. I can see from his face he never knew this part.

'Yeah,' I say to Stef, 'your brother done Kit.'

'She's chatting bare shit,' the girl says.

'No, I ain't. It's fully loaded facts, bro. Now sort this mess out,' I tell them and then I go. I'm just out the door and I can hear them saying how it's bullshit and Jamie and Kit were brothers and it don't make no sense.

As we're walking to the car, I say, 'Kieron, I wanna know who shot to Lauryn. And I know you fucking know something, so you better tell me, bro.'

Kieron looks away.

'Kieron! That's my sister, yeah? That's my fucking blood.'

Kieron lets out a deep sigh then he says, 'Rowmando.'

I turn and start to walk away, but Kieron grabs hold of me.

'Get your fucking hands off me, bro. Just allow it, Kieron.'

'He's a fucking youth, man.'

'Shut the fuck up,' I shout at him as I walk away.

I've got a temper. I fully admit it. I get angry quick and when I get angry I use my fists. When I'm angry, I forget my bad dreams and I forget my problems. When I'm in action, I ain't thinking morbid thoughts about Lauryn or what the fuck I should do about Sharon and all her cop aggression.

I come to Rowmando's auntie's door and rap it loud. I'm angry. I step back and look up at the window and I see Rowmando hiding behind the lace curtains looking down at me. He knows why I'm here. He's shitting himself.

I bang the door again. Rowmando's auntie answers.

'Is Row in?' I say.

'Rowmando's out,' she says, lying.

'Auntie, I've come to you respectfully and I'm asking you politely, but you're fucking lying,' I say to her. And then I shout, 'Row, get the fuck downstairs.'

'What do you want?' Auntie says. 'I can let him know.'

'It's got fuck all to do with you,' I tell her.

'Look, he's not in.'

I've had enough of her lies and push past her into the hallway just as Rowmando's coming down the stairs. When I see him, I just totally lose it. I catch him and throw him on the floor. I start screaming, that was my sister, that was my sister, that was my sister, and I'm punching the fuck out of him. He don't even try to fight back. He curls into a ball and tries to cover his face with his hands. He's crying, I mean really crying hard.

Auntie is trying to drag me off him.

'This child has suffered enough,' she says.

I look at the scars on Rowmando's face. When Jamie and the Fields mob were trying to dominate the Summerhouse mandem, one of the little tricks they played was to order up a delivery from us. Rowmando takes the order to a block of flats but instead of paying him for the drugs they threw acid in his face. The youth lost an eye and he's scarred for life. He's got a face like the hunchback of Notre Dame.

Auntie is pulling me off him, but she don't have to. I'm done.

'I was just shotting like you told me,' Rowmando sobs.

Auntie gets on the floor and hugs him as he cries.

I get up and go outside.

When I'm angry I forget about my problems. But then you do something angry which you regret and all your problems just come flooding back. Outside the house, I feel just as bad as I did after that time I punched Lauryn out.

I feel so bad and I don't know what to do about it. Not so long ago, I would of talked to Sully. He would understand. But Sully's got the Irish problem to deal with. And anyway, Sully's changed. Even if he didn't have the Irish to deal with, I don't know that he would of listened to me the way he used to.

Feels like everything's going to shit.

SIX MONTHS

Becks is a wise woman. She always talks total sense. But all that does is make me feel worse. Cos when you're wrong and you know you're wrong, you don't wanna hear the truth.

'Why are you even with me?' I ask her.

I'm serious. Cos right now I'm not liking myself.

Becks don't answer right off. She's thinking. She takes my hand.

And then she says, 'The first six months when you're with someone, there's all the excitement. Your hormones are running wild and your brain goes to mush. But after a while the brain and hormones get in balance again and that's when the hard work starts.'

'Are you saying I'm hard work?'

'There are people who only ever want the six months. They want that excitement. They want to fall in love over and over again because that's the easy part,' she says. 'It's being in a relationship that's hard work. If you're serious about wanting it to work, you have to roll up your sleeves. The question is, Jaq, do you want to make a go of this? Ask yourself that and be honest. Because I need to know.'

The mood I'm in, I don't know what to say.

'I hope the answer's yes,' she goes on, 'because that's what I want, more than anything in the world.'

I should say something. But sometimes with someone you love you can be childish. I just want to hold her and be held by her and for her to kiss me and tell me she loves me. And I would calm down. But instead I say, and I don't know why, I say, 'I don't know.'

Becks is so dignified. Everything about her is graceful. She doesn't shout or scream, she just nods slowly.

Then she says, 'I need to ask you something. Are you going to keep doing what you do? Can we talk about this?'

'I dunno, do I. It's all I've ever done. It's all I know how to do.'

'That's not true. You don't have to keep doing this. There are always options.'

'For you, yeah. There's always options when you come from money.'

'That's a cheap shot,' she says, hurt. 'But if you keep doing what you do, then I don't know how to help you.'

'You ain't gotta help me.'

'Somebody has to, because you need help. If you won't talk to me, there are other people who can help. People you can talk to. Counsellors. Therapists. There are people who can help take the pressure off.'

'I can't talk about what I do to no one, you know that.'

'Maybe we could find someone to look after baby Jack for a bit so you can have the space you need to heal.'

'What? He's my blood. He's my responsibility now.'

'Are you going to look after your nephew and push drugs

at the same time? How's that going to work?' She's not angry, she's not shouting. Becks doesn't do that. But she looks at me with the firm look.

I'm insulted. I am angry, I am shouting. 'Look, I do what I do.'

'What does that even mean?' she asks.

'You know what?' I say. 'I need some peace and fucking quiet here.'

Becks doesn't answer me for a minute. Then she says, 'All right, I'm going to give you some space.'

'A'right,' I say, still being childish. My heart is actually fucking breaking. I don't want space. I don't want peace and quiet. I want Becks. Why the fuck can't I just say that to the girl? Why do I have to be like this? It's like I'm on a railway line that's taking me somewhere I don't wanna go, but I can't stop and I can't get off.

She squeezes my hand and gets up. She leaves the room and comes back with a bag and starts to collect her stuff. I turn on the telly and watch it in a blank sort of way, pretending to ignore her except I'm aware of every move she makes. I try to concentrate on the TV and forget about what's going on between me and Becks. I'm taking in bits here and there, but I ain't fully listening. Then something comes on the news and I sit up straight and pay full attention. Two men shot dead in an old people's home. Both Irish. The first name I couldn't hear right, some weird Irish name. But the second name is Jonny. 'Jonny's my nephew in London. He'll be in touch with a time and place,' the smooth voice on the phone said that day me and Sully found the heads in the lorry. I turn the volume up so high it wakes baby Jack up and he starts crying.

'Baby Jack, not now,' I say, picking him up to comfort

him. 'This is Auntie Jackie's work. Auntie Jackie needs to see this.'

The TV does an interview with the daughter of one of the residents in the home. She's not happy about her old dad being caught up in a gunfight between two rival sets of gangsters. It says there is speculation that the killings are connected to a dispute over drugs and that the feds are following up a number of leads. But that's probably bullshit. It doesn't say if the rival gang that did the killing is Black or white. Whoever it was went in there to the old people's home were all ballied and gloved up. Normal.

Whoever it was. Ha. I know who it was. Sully. Stupid fucking Irish. They thought they could come in our ends and pull that kind of stunt? Nah, it ain't happening. They picked the wrong fella to piss off. My money was always on Sully.

I check my phones. The mandem are being very careful. One or two of them are posting links but no one's making any stupid comments that would attract the feds' attention.

I almost text Sully, but then I think that would be a fucking dumb thing to do. When things like this go down, the feds are listening out for chatter. I drop the phone on the sofa and lean back, hugging my knees, taking it all in.

Bad man Summerhouse Sully. That was his first real test as top boy since he took it away from Dushane and, fuck me, has he come through with flying colours. The man's a legend. I mean, he really is. There ain't no one who can get to Sully. That's why, in my opinion, Dushane ain't gone after him. Put Dushane against Sully, toe to toe, and there's only gonna be one winner.

I look at baby Jack and I say, 'Fuck me, baby Jack. The man is a legend.'

But baby Jack doesn't know what I'm talking about.

Becks is going round the place, picking up things she needs. I look back at the TV. Bullshit this, bullshit that. And then . . .

Fuck me.

No, seriously. Fuck me.

It's another crime story. A property developer called Jeffrey something, I don't even hear his second name. But I know exactly who he is. Found dead by the cleaner in his house. Police treating it as murder. Fuck me. This is big.

Jeffrey and his wife Lizzie were a right pair of hustlers. They started out with buy-to-lets, then expanded the business and were doing some big-scale property deals. They had Ps and they wanted more Ps. Which we all do. Ain't nothing wrong with that. Except the plan they come up with to grow their Ps was to get involved in the drug business. They didn't know anything about the business. They just thought they could make some very serious money out of it. So that's when they got into bed with Jamie. That's my little joke, cos Lizzie did literally get into bed with Jamie. The two of them mixed business and pleasure and had dreams of making several fortunes until Dushane and Sully interrupted things and brought them back to reality. No one was going to start any kind of competition against Dushane and Sully. They made that very clear.

With Jeffrey, Dushane saw an opportunity. The man knew the property game and Dushane needed to wash the money – which was literally millions – that he was making. So him and Jeffrey started doing business together. What I heard is that Dushane was investing in the Summerhouse redevelopment. At first, I found it hard to believe that

Dushane would join up with all them rich people to fuck his own community, throw them out of their homes and tear down the estate just to build fancy apartments for rich people. But then, when you think about it, the only thing Dushane has ever cared about is his money. So I figured it was probably true. Dushane and Jeffrey were in business together. And now Jeffrey was dead. What mysterious figure could of killed him? We all know business deals can go bad and people can get very angry. So when the TV says the police are treating it as murder, I'm naturally thinking of Dushane.

Becks appears with her laptop and a bag of her shit.

'I'm going to be at mine,' she says. 'If you want to talk. If you want to see me. Or if you need any help with baby Jack, or when social services get in touch, you know where I am.'

I could be grown here and tell Becks I don't want her to go. It's the last thing in the world I want. I could give her a sign. Just a small sign. Becks would see it cos she's that kind of person. And she understands me, even when I'm being like this. She would put her bag down and she would come and take my hand and she'd make everything OK. But she needs to hear some words. She needs to see some sign. And I don't give her nothing.

'You know what?' I say without even looking at her. 'I've got shit to do. Can you take baby Jack now?'

Becks doesn't say anything straight off.

I turn to her and I say, 'You said if I need any help with baby Jack. Well, I do. Can you take him?'

'I'll get his things,' she says.

She gets the baby's stuff together. Before she goes, she bends over and gives me a kiss I don't deserve. I act like

I don't notice it. As soon as she's out the door, I bust out crying. Why did I have to be like that? Why am I behaving like I'm seven years old?

Sharon's burner vibrates with a message. I read, Don't make me do something I don't want to do.

What the fuck's that supposed to mean?

I message her back. If you don't wanna do something. Simple. Don't do it.

You're not leaving me any choice.

I don't owe you nothing, I type.

You're leaving me no choice.

That's when I stop feeling sorry for myself. I'm angry now.

MARIANNE

I'm halfway to the market when it hits me how to put Sharon back in her box now Sully has sorted the Irish problem. I'll tell him all about her and the Dickie Simms stash. I was mad to think about doing it without telling him. That was a bad candidate. And like Jimmy the Indian always says, even when you've found a good move, you look for a better one. Telling Sully is the best move. If Sharon wants to play silly games, he will know how to fuck her up.

I turn the corner into the market and the first thing I see is Mandy with her shopping bags having a go at Kieron. I stop by a stall selling wigs and wait cos I don't want Mandy starting in on me.

'I can't believe this,' Mandy is saying to Kieron. 'You know what we did for you when Immigration came. We rolled out for you. Got ourselves dragged about by police. Put ourselves at risk. And this is how you repay us? You selling drugs to schoolkids now? I'm ashamed of you, bruv. I'm ashamed of all of you.'

Kieron's just sitting there taking it. He knows if it weren't for Mandy he'd be in fucking Rwanda right now. He can see Mandy's point. I can see Mandy's point. I can see why she's angry.

One of the youngers, Arlo, the fat cheeky kid, laughs and says, 'Listen to the Malcolm X fuckery.'

The youngers laugh but Kieron tells them to shut their mouths.

'You know about the protest tomorrow?' Mandy asks Kieron.

'Yeah.'

'Well, try to be there and support your community instead of fucking it up with this bullshit.'

Mandy turns and goes. She don't see me, thank fuck.

As I come up to Kieron I see Rowmando, back in his spot, shotting just like I told him to.

'Wagwan,' I say and I kind of nod at man as I pass and he don't know how to respond. He sort of looks away and hangs his head.

Romy and Kieron are looking at something on Romy's phone.

'You cool, cuz?' Romy asks me as I come up.

'I'm bless,' I say. 'Just people saying shit and pissing me off.'

'Anything needing dealing with?' Kieron asks.

'Nah, nah, nothing like that,' I say. 'Wagwan for the mandem, though. You lot been good?'

I ain't seen the youngers since Lauryn and they give me a good welcome.

'What you looking at?' I ask Romy.

Romy shows me the screen of his phone. He's on Tinder.

'Rah, this one's leng,' Kieron says, peeking at the phone. 'She's a little buff baddie still.'

‘I might have to superlike this one, you know,’ Romy says. ‘She’s brazy.’

‘I don’t know about superliking, though,’ I say. ‘She’s nice, but not a ten outta ten.’

‘Are you all right, cuz?’ Romy says. ‘She’s got no weave on and hardly no make-up. She’s on this natural mystics thing. I rate all of that. She’s getting my superlike, blood.’

‘But do you even link any of these girls, bro?’ I ask.

‘Don’t watch all that, cuz,’ he says with a naughty chuckle. ‘You don’t know what I do.’

Then I look over and I see Marianne, one of our regular clients, pushing her pram. She already has her money in her hand. Nitties are never cool. They can’t ever hide their need.

Rowmando is on her. ‘What I keep telling you, bro? Stop walking to us with the money out like that.’

I’m just about to start talking to Kieron and Romy about the killings in the old people’s home and also Jeffrey being murdered but then I hear Marianne tell Rowmando she wants some dark, and before I can say anything, I’m thinking about Lauryn and the time she bought her baggie of dark.

So I turn and watch Marianne and Rowmando.

Rowmando says, ‘Rah, you’re buying a lot this week. Where you getting your Ps from?’

‘Mind your business,’ she says.

Rowmando looks over at Kieron, who nods. So Rowmando takes her money and directs her over to the rubbish bags. Marianne pokes around, takes four cans and drops them into the pram.

‘Yo, Marianne,’ I call over to her. ‘One sec.’

'What now?' she says as I come up. 'I've paid him the money.'

'Just cool yourself, man,' I say.

I look in the pram. There ain't no baby. Just the cans with her dark covered by a stained pink blanket.

'Where's your baby?'

'What? Are you working for social services now or something?' she says, sarky.

'Stop chatting shit, bruv. I asked you a question. Where's your baby?'

'Don't worry about the baby,' she says.

It never makes a lotta sense questioning a crackhead. They'll tell you anything just to get their fix. If you get the truth, it's gonna be by accident.

I keep on at her. 'Where's your baby?'

'Baby's with my mum.'

'Your mum?'

'Yeah.'

'Where's your mum live?'

'Newham.'

'Where in Newham? What street?'

'Uh . . . I don't know the name of the street.'

'You don't know the name of the street where your mum lives? Where's your baby, bro?'

'I'm going to pick him up now.'

I'm getting a very bad feeling about this. She starts to push the pram but I stop her.

'You're gonna take me to your baby.'

'What?'

'You take me to see the baby and you can come back here and you get a lucky dip in the rubbish. Take whatever you can get with one hand.'

'Serious?'

'You heard what I said.' I call over to Rowmando, 'She gets a lucky dip, you hear me?'

Rowmando nods and looks away. He don't wanna look me in the eye. I feel like a bully. I feel very bad.

'Let's go Newham,' I say to Marianne.

'Nah, the baby's not in Newham, innit,' she says, and she laughs, like she's put one over on me.

'Yo, Kieron,' I say. 'Get the whip, man.'

Kieron ain't very happy having a nittie like Marianne and her horrible pram in his car, but I tell him I wanna see the baby.

Marianne lives in a high rise on Kingsmead and we're there in less than twenty minutes. I tell Kieron to wait in the car while I go inside with Marianne.

Even before Marianne opens the door I can hear the baby crying.

The place is just like I thought it would be, only worse. It's dirty and it's full of crap. Empty bottles all over the place. There's stains on the walls, on the floor and the chairs. You would not wanna sit down.

The kid's in a filthy white babygro. It's lying beside the cot where there's a lot of dirty old towels and blankets.

'Why's your fucking baby on the floor?' I ask her, but she ain't even thinking about the baby. She sits down on the sofa and starts fiddling with the cans to get the wraps out. Her hands are trembling.

'Pick up your child off of the floor,' I tell her.

She doesn't hear me.

I yell at her, 'Pick up your pickney off the floor.'

She gets up and picks up the baby. 'That's right,' she says to the child. 'Mummy's home. It's all right.'

She puts the baby into the cot.

'So this is how you're leaving your child, yeah?'

The baby is still crying. Marianne sits back on the sofa and goes back to the cans.

'Listen,' I shout at her. 'You ain't fucking smoking around your child. Go fucking sit in there and smoke your pipe, you tramp.'

She doesn't argue. She gets up and goes to the kitchen like I told her. All she wants is her fix.

I stare at the baby in the cot. His face is red. He smells. He needs changed. He needs washed. I look around at the squalor. I don't know what to do. I have no fucking idea.

So I leave.

When I get in the car, Kieron asks me where we're going. But I don't know. I start crying. Again. What the fuck is going on? All I'm doing these days is crying.

'What was all that about?' Kieron asks. 'Jaq? Are you all right?'

'This is so fucked, bro.'

'What's fucked?'

'Just take me to my place.'

On the way, to animate me, Kieron starts chatting about the Irish and how they got what was coming to them.

'I told you my money was on Sully,' I say.

'You were right.'

'Where was you this morning?' I ask him.

'What?'

'I'm assuming if Dushane and Sully got their food back, they've stashed it. So where did you meet them? Highbury or Stamford Hill?'

Kieron hesitates before telling me cos on the road it's need to know and, strictly speaking, I don't need to know where they're holding the food. Except I'm kind of Kieron's boss and if he can't trust me who can he trust? The world wouldn't make sense no more if he couldn't trust me.

So he says, 'Highbury.'

I know the exact house. It belongs to this posh white girl Antonia. Or it belongs to her dad and she lives in it. I ain't never seen her do a day's work, but she always has Ps. I guess Daddy gives her an allowance or whatever and I know Sully and Dushane are very generous with her when she's holding for us. It's worth it cos the feds are never going to raid her house looking for drugs. Antonia just ain't on their radar. The house is worth paying for.

'Why?' he asks.

'Nothing.'

We talk about Jeffrey, not naming no names. Kieron's mum was one of the ones on the estate along with Dushane's mum Pat and Ralph and all them who were trying to organise the tenants to stop the redevelopment, writing letters and petitions and that, so Kieron ain't got a lotta sympathy for Jeffrey. Him and the redevelopment fuckers pulled all kinds of tricks to get people out of their homes. They cut off the water, they cut off the electric. That's the kind of person Jeffrey was. So fuck him.

When we get to mine, he says, 'Listen, Jaq. I know bare people are coming up to you and saying that cliche shit when they've never been there for you. But you're my fucking family, and so was Lauryn, and I mean that shit. Anything happening, anything, just shout me, yeah? I'm being serious, you know. You sure you're going to be all right, though?'

'Yeah, I'll be sweet. A'right, bro. Love.'

'Love.'

I get out the car and go to my front door and get my keys out like I'm letting myself in. I wait for Kieron to drive off cos I don't want him to see me get in my own car.

And the why behind that is cos I've made up my mind.

I know what I have to do. It's funny cos it came to me in a flash. And I say it's funny cos given what a massive decision it is I didn't really consider it all that long. Can't lie, I've spent more time thinking about if I should buy a top or a pair of trainers than I did on making this decision. I know there are going to be consequences. They're gonna be very serious. And once it's done, there ain't no going back. Not for me.

This can only end one of two ways.

But I know I have to do it.

HELPING BABY JACK

I park under a tree across the street from the big house Antonia lives in. I can't tell if she's home, but I'm going to have to assume that she is, and that maybe even she has company. Nothing I can do about that. I take a good look around. It's quiet. For everyone living in the street, it's a normal evening. Nothing special going on. They're doing their normal shit. I'm the only one whose heart is racing. Even by my standards, what I'm about to do ain't normal.

I put the gloves on and slip the Glock into my pocket. I'm really hoping I don't have to take it out, let alone use it, cos I don't wanna have to hurt no one. But I also want to get what I've come for and I want to get away so there's a chance I will have to use the gun. Let's hope it don't come to that. I take the tyre lever from the boot and hide it inside my jacket.

I cross the road all casual like and quietly open the metal gate to the front garden. Down the side of the house there's a wooden door that leads into the back garden. Once I'm down the side and out of sight, I pull down the ballie, pull up the hoodie and take the lever from my jacket. The door's locked but it's only a Yale lock and it breaks easy.

There's steps down to the basement. I peer in through the glass panels on the back door. Can't see no one inside. I smash one of the small panes of glass. If it's belled up, I'm going have to be very quick. But no alarm goes off, which probably means Antonia's at home. I wait a minute and listen, just in case there's anyone inside who might of heard the breaking glass. My heart is thumping, but no one comes running to see what's going on, so I reach inside and open the door. That's when I hear music playing and Antonia's voice. She's on the phone, to one of her mates sounds like. Fuck, the bitch can talk, which is good for me, her stupid chat and the music.

I've been in the house three or four times and I know exactly where they keep the food. It's in a small broom closet at the foot of the stairs. They've fastened it with a padlock. Even small padlocks can be hard to break unless you've got the right tools, which I don't have. I have to make more noise than I want because it takes two or three goes with the tyre lever before it breaks. I pause a second and listen out. Antonia's still talking, but her tone sounds different now, kind of guarded. She ain't chatting normal. I think she's heard something. I gotta get what I came for and get out fast.

The two bags are hidden behind a vacuum cleaner and some boxes of junk. I open one of them just to make sure. Bricks of white. This is what I came for. I sling the bags on my shoulder. They're heavy. I would guess around ten to fifteen kilos each.

Just as I'm heading to the back door, Antonia comes creeping down the stairs, this what's-going-on? look on her face. When she sees me, she turns and tries to run back up the stairs. I grab her foot and pull her down. She's fighting me all the way and I have to crack her over the head with the butt of the pistol. She's not totally unconscious, but she is dazed. I grab some clothesline from the closet, tie her to the banisters at the foot of the stairs and I'm out of there.

I throw the two bags into the boot, jump in the car and drive off. Antonia won't be calling the feds. I mean, what's she gonna say to them? Please, officer, a horrible, nasty burglar came and stole these drugs I was holding for man? Nah. She ain't gonna do that. It's not the feds I'm worried about. Antonia won't be calling them. But as soon as she gets out of the clothesline she will be calling Sully to tell him his stash has been robbed. All I can do is pray that she ain't recognised me.

No sensible drug dealer will spend any more time than is absolutely necessary in a car with drugs and straps for the simple reason that the feds stop totally innocent Black people in their cars all the time. My car is totally legit, it's registered and insured. Lithe insisted on everything being done correct. But that never stops the feds. It's just common sense. If you don't wanna get caught in possession, don't be in possession any longer than you have to be, innit. But here I am, driving round, and I realise now I don't have a plan. I did not think this through. I do not know what I'm doing or where I'm going. I'm just driving. And that's a madness. I gotta think things through. I gotta come up with a plan. What would Jimmy say? What's my best move here? What are my candidates?

I have no fucking idea.

I keep driving. Every time a police car passes it's kind

of weird, but it's like I can't see nothing except what's right in front of me. I can't see anything to the side. All I can see is this narrow tunnel ahead of me and I'm focusing on getting to the end of that tunnel. And I can hear fucking everything, including my own heart hammering in my chest. I'm going to have to come up with a fucking move quick. I can't just drive round like this all night.

I pull over and call Kieron. 'Yo, cuz. Where are you?'

'Home, with my mum.'

'I need to see you urgently, bro.'

'A'right?' Kieron sounds suspicious.

'Meet me by the garages in the ends in what, twenty?'

'A'right.'

'A'right. Cool. Say less.'

It takes me ten minutes to get to the garages. While I'm waiting for Kieron, I think about what I've just done. What have I just done? I've just robbed Sully and Dushane's food. That ain't something you can just say you made a mistake and apologise for. That is instant death. I know that. I should be sorry, but I ain't. I had to do it.

Kieron arrives. 'Wagwan. You hear about Dushane?'

'Nah, what?'

'The feds are after him for murder.'

'Fuck me. Jeffrey? It was Dushane done him?'

'That's what the feds are saying. It's been on the news.'

Part of me is thinking this could be good for me. If the feds are looking at him for murder, Dushane ain't gonna have a lotta time to worry about getting his food back.

'What did you want to see me for?' Kieron asks.

I open the boot. Kieron looks inside. He recognises the two bags straight off. He looks at me and says, 'Sully never said nothing about having to move it.'

'This ain't got nothing to do with Sully,' I say.

Kieron never reacts quick. He's a careful guy and always takes a second to think things through before he speaks. First, he gets this puzzled look on his face. Then the penny drops and he's horrified. And terrified.

Before he says anything, my phone rings. It's Sully. Kieron looks at me. It rings and rings. I let it ring out.

'What are you doing, bro?' Kieron asks.

'It's too late to help Lauryn,' I say. 'But it ain't too late to help baby Jack.'

He looks at me like I'm mad. Then his phone rings. He holds up the screen for me to see. Sully.

'I need to answer this, Jaq,' he says.

I nod. Kieron licks his lips, steps back a little and answers. 'Yo?'

I can't hear what Sully's saying, but I can guess. Kieron glances at me nervously.

'What?' Kieron says, trying to sound surprised. 'No. No.' And again, 'No, course not, bruv.' Then finally, 'A'right.'

He ends the call and looks at me in a way I never seen him look at me before. There's some annoyance in there. Maybe even anger.

'Did Sully say anything about me?' I ask.

'No,' he says.

'Who does he think done it?'

'He don't know yet. But, trust me, he's gonna find out. You need to give this back to both of them man, Sully and Dushane. They own half each.'

'I can't do that.'

'Yes, you can, Jaq. You need to give it back and tell them you're sorry and you don't know what you were thinking. Tell him your mind got distracted cos of Lauryn and you didn't know what you were doing.'

'But I do know what I'm doing, Kieron man. I do. I'm taking this shit off the streets so it won't kill no one else.'

'Jaq, there's always gonna be shit on the streets. If it ain't ours, it'll be someone else's.'

'Yeah, but we don't have to be involved in it no more.'

He looks at me like I've lost my mind. He says, 'When Sully finds out it was you, he's gonna kill you. And if he don't, Dushane will.'

'You gonna tell Sully?'

Kieron swallows hard and breathes in deep.

'Are you?' I ask again.

'You're my blood, Jaq. I ain't gonna tell him. But what you've done, coming to me, showing me this, you're putting my life on the line, innit. Cos by rights I should of told Sully it was you when he called. The fact I didn't tell him, that makes me just as guilty as you.'

'This ain't on you, bruv.'

'It is now. You've put it on me. It was me told you the stash was in the Highbury house. I just told Sully I don't know who took it. What do you think Sully's gonna do when he finds out I lied to him?'

'He ain't gonna find out. I ain't gonna tell him and neither are you, right?'

Kieron shakes his head. 'I gotta get home,' he says. 'My mum's got this swelling on her stomach, fluid. It's called ascites. It's very uncomfortable for her. I gotta get the doctor to drain it.'

'Go be with your mum,' I say. 'Tell her bless from me.'

He throws me a look. 'Jaq, this is so fucked up. Tell Sully. Do it now. Make it right.'

'Nah, man,' I say. 'This shit has gotta stop.'

I watch Kieron get back in his car. My phone rings. It's Becks. I don't know if I should answer it.

'Yo?' I say.

'How are you?' Becks says.

'I'm good.'

'Good. Um . . . listen, I'm sorry to bother you, but Sharon has been calling me. She wants to talk to you.'

Sharon the fucking fed. What the fuck? Whoever invented the saying it never rains but it pours knew what he was talking about. It's raining so hard I'm drowning here.

'She ain't got no right to be calling you,' I say.

'She says it's urgent. She really needs to talk to you.'

'Sharon can go fuck herself,' I say.

'She says she wants to help you.'

'Help me?' I say, sarcastic. 'That bitch?'

'Jaq, is everything all right?'

'Couldn't be better.'

'Do you want me to come over?'

'No. Don't come to the house.'

I don't want her anywhere near the house. I'm thinking of Sully. I don't want to put her in danger. But Becks misunderstands what I'm saying, as if I don't wanna see her. She's quiet for a moment, then she says in a small voice, 'All right.'

'I've got something going on,' I say. 'It's complicated.'

'What is it?'

'I can't explain. Not now. Don't worry about it.'

'I am worried. About you.'

'Don't be. I can look after myself. How's baby Jack?'

'He's sleeping. He misses you.'

'Baby Jack misses me? Did he tell you that himself, did he?' I say, being a fucking horrible bitch.

Becks doesn't answer straight off. Then she says, 'If you need anything, Jaq, you know where we are.'

'I don't need anything,' I say, and I hang up.

Still acting like a seven-year-old.

What's my best move?

ALL THE TOP BOY GHOSTS

I've fucked myself. I've taken man's food, and there's gonna be a price to pay. I could tell Sully everything and say I'm sorry. Tell him I wasn't thinking straight after Lauryn. And, I dunno, maybe Sully would give me a pass. He might. But if he let me live, he wouldn't trust me no more the way he used to, and I'd have to think about how to earn my Ps going forward. I've been on the road since I was fourteen years old. I ain't never done nothing else. It's all I know. If I can't work on the road, what the fuck am I supposed to do? What jobs are out there for someone like me? Shelley would give me a job in the nail bar, but it would be outta pity cos I don't know nothing about nails. I don't find nails, specially other people's nails, that interesting, can't lie. Certainly not interesting enough to make it my career the way Shelley has.

I'm in bed. Of course I can't sleep. Everything's going round in my head. It's making me sick. I am so fucked.

Sooner or later Sully's gonna come looking for me and he's gonna ask me direct, Jaq, did you take the grub from the Highbury house? What am I gonna say to man? Am I gonna look him in the eye and lie to him? Cos I don't think I can do that. Man will see I'm lying and then there ain't no doubt about what happens next.

Calling Sully now and confessing to him is probably the best chance I have of staying alive. And even that chance ain't that big. Even it was big, problem is I don't want the drugs out there. I don't want another Lauryn. I don't wanna see another baby lying on the floor in a filthy babygro. I don't wanna see another kid like Rowmando lose an eye. I don't want baby Jack going on the road. I don't want him to end up in jail or dead.

I start thinking about all the people I know who died cos of this shit. I'm lying there in the dark and I say their names out loud, like counting sheep. Maybe it'll put me to sleep.

Lee Greene is the first one I can think of. He was before my time, but I'm thinking far back, thinking of everyone I ever knew or heard of. All the top boy ghosts. Lee worked for Bobby Raikes. His brother has the dry cleaner's opposite Summerhouse and he's a nice man. Maybe Lee was nice too, I don't know. But he's dead. Couple of mysterious figures laid him out just as Sully and Dushane were taking over the business from Bobby Raikes. So that's one I can think of.

Bobby Raikes is two. Maybe only one and a half cos Bobby Raikes weren't from our community. He was just making money off us. Just like I am, I suppose, so maybe he counts as a full number. He ran things in Summerhouse till another so-called mysterious figure laid him out. That's two.

Who else?

Dris. Dris is definitely a full number. He was a single dad to Erin all the time Mandy was in the pen. He was a good dad. He was always there for Erin. It was Dris who recommended me to Dushane when Dushane came back from Jamaica. If it hadn't been for him, I wouldn't of rose up the ranks the way I did. Dris makes three.

There was this little kid Michael who hero-worshipped Dushane. During the war with the Albanians, Dushane was on his way home not knowing that the Albanians were waiting for him in his flat. Michael got out on the balcony and shouted to Dushane that the Albanians were hiding in his yard. They tossed him over the side. Michael was about twelve years old. Four.

Leon. Leon liked to help people. He tried to help Ra'Nell when Ra'Nell's mum Lisa was in the nuthouse. Tried to keep him away from the road. Leon got stabbed up in the flats. Five.

Dushane's cousin Donovan got killed in Jamaica cos of something Dushane done there involving this big gangster Sugar. Six.

Attica. I don't like thinking about Ats cos it was me lured him in, trying to get to Stef and Jamie. Ats' mum Amma lost her job at the hospital and Ats wanted to step up and be the big man bringing home the Ps for her. The workmen found him dumped in a skip. Amma got deported. Seven.

Turned out Ats got killed cos Kit didn't like the way he was disrespecting Stef. Kit got someone to bad him up, but that someone went too far and it all went wrong. Eight.

Jason got torched down there in Ramsgate or wherever it was. It was racists what done that, but Jason wouldn't of been in the house when they firebombed it if Sully hadn't of brought him there. Nine.

That girl Tilly who was waiting to meet Jamie to go on a date when there was the drive-by. They were trying to get Jamie but they missed and got Tilly instead. She worked in Westfield, totally innocent. If Jamie hadn't been in Westfield to have a serious talk to Cam and the A Road mob, she would still be alive. Ten.

Michael. He was just a little kid. No, wait. I already counted Michael. Who else is there? Jamie, of course. Jamie had big plans. I never liked him but I ain't just counting the people I liked. Eleven.

Ricky, who was a friend of Sully's. They stopped at a petrol station when they were looking for Jamie except Jamie and Kit found them first and Ricky got killed. Twelve.

Modie, who used to run the Fields mandem. The feds got him, shot him dead in his car after he busted outta jail. Thirteen.

Haze, who worked in London for Sugar and the Jamaicans. He got laid in his car. Fourteen. And Sugar got poisoned in his jail cell, so he's fifteen.

Kamale, who had a beef with Dushane and Sully back when they were still working for Bobby Raikes and Lee Greene. Kamale got buried alive is what I heard. Sixteen.

Them two Moroccans whose heads we found. I can't remember their names, but that's another two. Brings us up to eighteen.

Dushane's old partner from back in the day, Joe. The Albanians shot him dead. Nineteen.

Dushane's other partner Jeffrey. I don't know if he

belongs on this list, but he'd probably still be alive if he hadn't met Dushane. Twenty.

Dushane's brother Chris. He didn't die, but during some argument about food or Ps or whatever shit some people broke into Chris's house looking for Dushane. They put the iron on and they ironed Chris's chest. He had to have a lot of surgeries over the years to get that fixed and I don't think they ever fixed it right. And Chris was a total civilian. He works in an estate agent's. His only crime was he's Dushane's brother.

Who else?

Cam, of course. Jamie threw him off a tower block when Cam was trying to block Jamie's Zero Tolerance thing. Is that twenty? Twenty-one? I'm losing count.

I suppose if you're counting the opps there's also the two Irish, Jonny and the other fella. Then there's the Turks that Jamie and Kit firebombed. And the Albanians from Green Lanes who tried to take on Dushane and Sully.

There's more, if we're including all the opps, including the time when Sully got kidnapped, and I was one of the ones who went in to get him back. There was three fellas in there holding Sully. None of them man made it out alive.

I can't remember any more. Anyway, I've lost count.

Wait, what the fuck. I'm forgetting Lauryn.

'Lauryn, I'm sorry,' I say. 'How could I forget you?'

Tears roll down my cheeks and make the pillow wet. How could I forget Lauryn? Is that twenty or twenty-one or twenty-two? Or thirty? I don't know.

You could say most of them deserved what they got. They were roadmen. They were doing bad things. Except no one's just a roadman. They're also a son, a daughter, a brother, a sister, a father, a mother, a friend, a partner. No one's just one thing. And even if they did some wrong things, they probably also did some good things in their lives for the people they loved.

The top boy ghosts.

All very different. The one thing they have in common is they'd all be alive if it wasn't for what we do on the road. We do our thing, sell our food, make our Ps, and we leave this trail of wreckage behind us that we don't even think about.

Except now I'm thinking about it.

How did I get here? Where did this start?

Was it fucking Mandy? Did Mandy put this in my head chatting shit about Angela Y. Davis and the Irishwoman Bernadette and the rest of them political people? Did it start that day when the Immigration came looking for Kieron? When the feds let him go, when Kieron stepped outta the van, it felt very good, can't lie. It's the only time I can ever remember where the community rolled out to support someone. And we won. That don't happen every day.

The community came out to support us and we turn round and fuck it. Just like Mandy says we do.

I could call Sully now and tell him it was me who took the bags. I could beg him to give me a pass. That's probably my best chance.

But I don't want to take it.

BRUV, WE HAVE A SITUATION

I'm getting outta the shower when I get a text from Kieron. He's just come outta the Highbury house with Sully, Dushane and Junior. He's told them he thinks it's Si and the Fields mandem who took the food. They're on their way to the Fields now.

My heart starts banging.

If Kieron persuades Sully that Si stole the food, then maybe there's a chance for me. Si might die for something he didn't do. But better him than me, I'm thinking, can't lie. I never liked him anyway. He'll be number thirty-three or four or five. Fuck, this food is killing us, it really is.

I dry off and go to get dressed. Except when I lie down on the bed just to get myself together, I fall asleep.

My phone pings with a text and wakes me up. It's Kieron. It weren't Si. He's with Sully and they're coming to mine. He says to get out fast.

I jump and get dressed double-quick.

As I'm leaving, I take a last look at my yard. I never thought I'd ever live somewhere this nice, that I'd own somewhere like this. I love my house. I love living here.

When I close the door I ain't sure I'm ever gonna see it again.

I jump in the car and head for Becks'.

My phone rings. Sully. My blood runs cold. I don't answer. He leaves a voice message: Jaq, I'm outside your house. What's going on? Call me back.

He knows. He knows it was me. I can hear it in his voice. I call Becks. She doesn't pick up. I leave a voice message: Becks, listen. I'm going to be outside yours in twenty minutes, yeah? Have the baby ready. Get whatever you need for a few days, all right? Listen, I'm not fucking about. I need you to be ready. Twenty minutes, yeah?

There's a text from Sully: Bruv, we have a situation. Call me asap.

I know the next place Sully will come looking for me will be Becks'. I try Becks again but she still doesn't answer. I don't wanna break the speed limit cos if I get stopped with the strap and the drugs in the boot I'm truly fucked. But if I don't get to Becks before Sully, it's not just me that's fucked. It's Becks and maybe even baby Jack too. Yeah. You don't believe Sully would go that far? You don't know Sully. If his food is at stake, he will do whatever it takes.

I wish I could call Kieron, but if he's in a car with Sully, which I'm assuming he is, it would not be cool and he wouldn't be able to talk anyway. All I would be doing is putting Kieron in more danger than I already put him. When I got him to tell me where the food was and then showed him the bags in my car, he was right. I was making him an accomplice. If Sully finds me, he's gonna suspect Kieron. I hope Kieron is deleting his messages cos Sully will want to see his phone.

At that exact moment, my phone rings. It's Kieron. I almost answer it cos I'm desperate to know what he knows. But I catch myself in time and let it ring out. I can't even be sure it is Kieron. It might be Sully on Kieron's phone, for all I know.

When I get to Becks' place, I knock the door cos I've left my set of keys at home. Becks eventually comes to let me in. She's got baby Jack in her arms and her phone clamped to her ear. She looks at me puzzled.

'Hang up the phone,' I say.

She turns from me and says into the phone, 'Sorry, John. Can I give you a call back in thirty? Thanks. OK. Sorry.'

'Where's your stuff?' I say.

'What stuff?'

'I messaged you telling you to get everything together.'

'Jaq, I've been on work calls all morning. What's wrong with you?'

'We need to leave.'

She frowns. 'What are you talking about?

'I'm going to grab a few bits for the baby,' I tell her. 'Please just go and get what you need.'

'What the fuck are you talking about?'

'Just go.'

'You're scaring me, Jaq.'

'Becks, I don't have time for this right now. Please go and grab a few bits for a few days. We need to leave now. Now! Fuck, man.'

I take baby Jack while she goes off to get her bits.

'Be quick,' I say.

I'm holding baby Jack in one hand and gathering up his bottles, nappies and clothes. Then I go to the window and look out for Sully's car. This must of been what

Rowmando was feeling when he saw me banging on his door.

Why is Becks taking so long?

'Becks,' I yell. 'Hurry up, man.'

She comes downstairs all flustered.

'Are you ready?' I say. 'We have to leave.'

'Wait, wait,' she says. 'I need my laptop.'

'No, you don't. Come on. Let's go.'

'Jaq, I need my laptop.'

She goes off to get her computer and all the cables. I'm doing my nut.

Eventually, she's got everything she needs. We take the bags and the baby seat out to the car and load up.

'When are you going to tell me what's going on?' Becks asks.

'Get in the car, babe.'

Becks gets in the back with baby Jack. I start the engine and I've just turned into a side road when I see in my rear-view mirror Sully and Dushane pulling up in two cars, along with Junior and Kieron. I drive on, fast.

'Where are we going?' Becks asks.

All my criminal instincts are screaming at me that it's only a matter of time before the feds pull me over and find the food and the strap. That's a lot of time in jail. They might offer me a deal if I snitch, but that ain't never gonna happen. Sully's gonna kill me when he finds me, but I would never snitch on him. Never. That probably don't make a lot of sense to people who live normal lives. But if you have my life, if you work on the road, you know there is nothing lower than a snitch. I'd rather be in jail.

Becks keeps on at me. Where are we going? What are we doing? What's happened?

I pull over and stare straight ahead through the windscreen.

'I've done something dumb,' I say.

'All right,' Becks says. 'Whatever it is, we'll figure it out.'

'Nah, there ain't no going back from this one. I'm so sorry I got you involved.'

'Tell me what's going on.'

'I've got twenty-five kilos in the boot. I stole it from Sully and Dushane and they know it was me and now they're after me. If they catch me, I'm dead.'

I can see Becks in the rear-view mirror trying to take this in.

'Well,' she says, 'can you speak to them? Explain that with Lauryn and everything . . .'

'Nah, it don't work like that, babe.'

'Why did you steal it?'

'Lauryn died cos of this shit. This shit needs to stop now.'

Becks doesn't know what to say. Neither of us does. We sit in silence for a couple of minutes.

'How long are we going to have to hide for? A week?'

'Maybe a little longer.'

'How long?'

'I don't know.'

'What kind of life is the baby going to have on the run, Jaq?'

I don't have an answer for her.

'Jaq?'

'It's gonna be all right. A'right, babe?'

She ain't convinced. 'Where are we going, Jaq? Because I have a job. I have clients who depend on me. I can't just disappear on them.'

'I said it's going to be all right.'

'How is it going to be all right?'

I still don't have an answer.

She says, 'Should we think about going to the police?'

'No,' I shout back at her. 'That ain't happening. No police.'

'Could Mandy help?'

'No, Mandy can't help.'

'What about Kieron?'

'I've already asked too much from Kieron. I've put him at risk.'

'Then what are we going to do?'

I'm quiet a long time. I'm working through my candidates, searching for the best move. Baby Jack gurgles in his car seat and Becks gives him his bottle.

I put the car in gear and drive to Becks' dad Robert's house. Sully don't know where Robert lives or that he even exists. Becks and baby Jack will be safe there, at least until I get this sorted out.

When we get to Robert's, I help unload the car. Robert watches from the door. I don't imagine this is what he ever wanted for his daughter. She's gay, that probably wasn't a welcome surprise. She's going out with a girl from Summerhouse. The only time he would of heard of Summerhouse probably was on the news when there was a murder. And now his daughter is arriving home with a baby that ain't hers and whose mum died of an overdose. I don't think Robert had that plan in mind for Becks.

He ain't even helping to take Becks' bits inside. He just stands in the door staring at me. It's a what-the-fuck-are-you-doing-with-my-daughter? look. He thinks I'm trash, I can see it in his eyes.

Becks comes back to the car and kisses me. I'll bet it's killing Robert to see his daughter do that.

Becks says, 'You know I love you?'

'I love you too, babes. I'm just sorry I got you involved in this shit.'

I give the little king a kiss. 'You'll soon be home with Auntie Jackie and Auntie Becks,' I tell him. He grabs my little finger and gurgles.

'Do you like dogs?' I ask Becks.

'What?'

'You told me you like dogs, didn't you?'

'I love dogs. We had a Border collie when I was a kid. She was so smart. Why?'

'Cos I want us to have a dog. Maybe two. And for us to live in a cottage in the country. It's my dream. It's what I see for us. What do you think?'

'It's a very nice dream,' she says with a smile. 'As long as there's a good internet connection.'

'I'm gonna fix this situation and I'm gonna make that dream happen,' I say.

I watch her go back up to the house, baby Jack in her arms. She turns to wave at me then disappears inside. Robert closes the door behind them.

I really hope I see her again. But I don't know if I will.

As I drive east, back to the ends, I make a call to an old friend.

THE FOOD IS KILLING US

Jimmy is waiting on the canal by the lock gates where he said he'd be. He grins as I come up, flashing his superwhite teeth and he gives me a kiss. He keeps the big smile plastered all over his face even though he can obviously see I'm mad stressed. He twists his rings, starting with the little finger of his left hand, and I tell him everything.

'If I give Sully and Dushane their food back, there's a chance I could get a pass,' I say.

'From both Sully *and* Dushane?'

'If Sully gives me a pass, Dushane ain't gonna go against him, long as he gets his food back. But the thing is I don't want this shit in our community no more. There's just too many people dying and I don't wanna be part of it no more. Specially not after Lauryn.'

Jimmy nods slow. He ain't smiling now.

'What's my candidates?' I ask him.

'I'm sorry to say this, Jaq, but sometimes there are no candidates. There is only one move and it's forced.'

'So what's my move?'

Jimmy checks that there ain't no one listening in to our

conversation. He looks at me very serious. 'I think you already know what the move is,' he says. 'Sully has to go.'

Fuck me.

Sully has to go.

Yeah, I'd be lying if I said I hadn't already considered that possibility. But in my mind it was a candidate that was very low down on the list.

'I've crossed paths with Sully a couple of times,' Jimmy says. 'He's damaged goods. I don't know the details of what he's been through, or what he's done, or what he's had done to him. But what I see is a very damaged human being.'

I tell him about Jason and how Jason got burned to death in front of Sully's eyes, and how sometimes long after the fire you'd see Sully sniffing his hands for the smoke he said he could still smell on his fingers.

'That must have been very hard for him,' Jimmy says. 'Sometimes when life throws a lot of difficult challenges at you, some people shut down parts of themselves and their emotions. They don't want complexity because that takes them into parts of their heads where they don't want to go. What they want is simplicity because that way they don't have to interrogate themselves, they don't have to examine painful things, or relive their regrets. Everything has to be simple. It's easier to deal with. And here, in this specific case, the simple solution for Sully is for him to kill you. That's what he'll be thinking. A hundred per cent.'

Course, I already knew that Sully would be thinking that, but hearing it from Jimmy is like a kick in the stomach.

'Sully demands total loyalty,' Jimmy says. 'He has to. His life and freedom depend on it. If someone betrays him, they have to die. It's that simple. He sees the world in black and white. It's the only way his world can make sense to him. He knows he's either beast or prey. In Sully's world, you kill or be killed.'

I can't say anything cos I know he's right. I just look out over the water. There's swans and ducks and some people are throwing them bread.

'The question for you,' Jimmy says, 'is are you going to wait for him to make his move or are you going to move first?'

'I don't know if I can do that,' I say.

'You mean you don't think you can get to him?'

'No, I don't know if I could pull the trigger.'

'Why not?'

'I love the man.'

Jimmy don't laugh or make a face or nothing.

'He's been more than good to me,' I say.

'I understand that,' he says. 'But if you don't pull the trigger on him, he'll pull it on you.'

I know he's right. But that don't make it easier.

'Jaq,' Jimmy says, 'I'm glad you've come to me. You know I'm here for you.'

'Bless,' I say. 'Thank you.'

'What do you want to do?' he asks. 'About this problem?'

I shrug.

He leans in and says in a whisper, 'If you want, I'll do it.'

Fuck me.

I just stare down at my hands. I don't know what to say.

'Your mum has been living with me for nearly two years

now. It's not always easy, with Violet. She has her ups and downs. But when her head is in the right place, we get on very well.'

'Lemme see,' I say.

He shows me a couple of photos on his phone. Mum looks just like Lauryn. Same eyes, same shape face. She's smiling in the pictures, though to me she still looks like a troubled woman. A troubled woman who's smiling for the camera.

'You make her happy,' I say.

'I want to keep it that way,' he says. 'Which means this problem you have with Sully is my problem also.'

I get a call. Kieron. I really want to talk to man but I don't know if it's him. It could be Sully using his phone or Sully could be listening in. Jimmy looks at me: are you gonna answer that? I let it ring out.

It rings again straight after. Kieron.

'Yeah?' I say, very careful.

'Jaq, it's me.'

'A'right. You alone?'

'Yeah.'

'What's going on?'

'Sully and Dushane know it's you.'

'What are they saying?'

'You can imagine. They want their grub back. Dushane's doing his nut. Man's desperate cos of this problem with the feds and the murder.'

'Did they say what they were gonna do?'

'Sully says it all depends on you. But the longer you play this game of hide and seek, the harder it's gonna be when he finds you.'

'I'll talk to man,' I say.

'I just left him in the Number One Caff,' he says.

'You think I should talk to him?'

'I don't see you've got no choice.'

'A'right,' I say. 'Thanks for calling.'

'Sweet,' he says and I hang up.

Sully's in the top boy office. If it was anyone else except Kieron, I would think it's a set-up. I walk in there and bang! It's all over. But Kieron wouldn't do that to me.

Would he?

'I gotta go,' I say to Jimmy.

'Say the word, Jaq,' Jimmy says, 'and I'll take care of this for you.'

'I appreciate what you're offering, Jimmy. I really do. But I don't want Sully to die cos of this. I just don't want this shit to be killing us no more.'

'All right,' he says. 'Listen, one more thing before you go. Your dad wants to see you.'

I didn't mean to, obviously, it's so embarrassing, but I bust out crying. I didn't have nothing to wipe my eyes or my nose. I was making a big mess of myself. I turn away from Jimmy so he can't see what a wreck I am.

He taps me on the shoulder and passes me this big gentleman's handkerchief. I blow into it. It's so noisy, it's like a fucking trumpet.

'Sorry about your hankie,' I say.

'Don't be sorry, that's what it's for,' Jimmy says with a laugh. 'Have another good blow. Go on.'

'My dad wants to see me?' I ask him.

'It took a while, but I managed to get through to Vincent and tell him about Lauryn. He was shocked. I told him that you'd like to be in touch with him and he said he wants that.'

'He does? He said that?'

'Yes. He says to tell him when Lauryn's funeral is going to be and he'll come over. He said he really wants to see you.'

Now my head is going all over the place. I get this ridiculous idea that if I tell Sully my dad's coming over to see me, he'll give me the pass cos he'll understand how important it is to me.

Unfortunately, meeting my dad after all these years is not as important as Sully's food.

'Do you have a picture of him?' I ask.

Jimmy shows me a selfie he took with Dad in the restaurant in Toronto.

'He looks like he could do with eating a bit more healthy,' I say.

'Vincent was always skinny, but he's doing OK.'

'And he's really gonna come over?'

'That's what he said.'

'Do you believe him?'

'I do. He talked about you a lot. He really wants to see you.'

I wipe my eyes and my nose and hold out the hankie for him.

'You can hold on to that,' he says.

'I gotta go,' I say.

'If you change your mind,' he says, twisting his rings, 'tell me and I will take care of Sully. In the meantime, be careful.'

When Jimmy gives you a hug, he's so strong, he holds you so tight. You feel safe.

But hugs always have to end, don't they? The other person always lets you go. Just the way it is. Cos really we're on our own.

At the end of the day, we have to take care of our problems on our own.

GOING LONG

I park in the supermarket car park where I know the fella. He never charges me cos I give him a baggie of weed every now and then. The two bags are in the boot. I leave them, but I take the Glock. I check the safety then slide the gun into the waistband of my trousers at the small of my back. If you're the kind of person who has never carried a strap, then you won't know about having that feeling, something cold and hard and lethal pressing at the base of your spine. It makes you feel ten foot tall.

And I need to feel big for what I'm about to do.

I cross the road to the Number One Caff. I look in the window and see Sully sitting alone at a table. He looks very tired.

'Are you taking the piss?' he says when I walk in.

'Can I sit?'

He looks at the chair opposite and I sit.

'Why did you do it?' he asks. 'I know you took it. Don't lie to me.'

'I wouldn't lie to you, ever.'

'Course not, just steal. You still got it? Every bit of it?'

'Yeah.'

'The only reason I ain't done already deleted the fuck outta you – right here, right now – the only reason is cos when I was on the boat, when there was things going on in my head, you were there for me. You were the one person I actually wanted to see. I let you come on my boat. You were in my place, you were in my space. I invited you in. And now you do this to me?'

'There's bare shit going on in my head, Sully, you know? I'm looking around and nothing is making sense to me. All I know is I don't wanna be doing this shit no more.'

'Then don't. But you took my food and that ain't your choice to make.'

'The food is killing us. It's killed Lauryn. How many more of us need to go?'

'Shush,' he says. 'Lauryn killed herself. Don't blame me.'

'I'll bring you your food back.'

'Oh yeah, you will. Don't worry about that. And don't go making it sound like you've got any other option, cos you don't. You was there for me, but that only buys you so much. You took something that weren't yours to take. That ting comes back to me today.'

'All I'm asking for is a guarantee. A pass.'

'Shut up about guarantees. You sound like you think you're in the position to propose deals and it's starting to piss me off. Where's my shit?'

'I'll bring it, I swear down.'

'I want it tonight.'

'I know the next time I see you, you're going to decide whether I live or die. I know that. But, Sully, I'm begging you, please, don't hurt my family. Becks and the baby have no part in this.'

'I ain't giving no guarantees. I want my food and I want it tonight. And I don't want no excuses.'

'I want Dushane there and all,' I say. 'Half of it's his. And, no offence, I know you and him have a beef, and if I give you the two bags and he don't get his, he's gonna hold me responsible for that, not you. And I need to be in the clear with both of youse.'

Sully looks at me like he's not impressed. He leans back in his chair like he don't have a care in the world.

I saw this documentary one time years ago on the TV about cats. Me and Lauryn watched it together. Lauryn was mad about cats. We had so many kittens when we was young, but then after Mum started going missing we didn't have enough money to buy them their food, and if cats don't get fed, they don't hang around. On this documentary, it was about these cats living in some kind of lorry park. Feral cats, they were called. Anyway, these cat lovers saw how scrawny and dirty and full of disease they all were and decided to round them up and vaccinate them, feed them up and cut their bits off. But the trouble was trying to catch them, even if it was for their own good. So what they did, they got these experts in who catch feral animals in traps. And what I remember from the documentary was the main expert saying that the nursing females are the hardest to get. Cos they have a litter to look after, they're cautious. The nursing females would sniff around the trap and they didn't like it at all. But the dominant tom cat, the alpha male, it turns out, is the easiest to catch. That surprised me. I thought the big bad tom would be the hardest to catch, but apparently he's the easiest because he's the king of the castle. He's the top boy and he ain't afraid of nothing. So the tom just strolls into the trap, not expecting anything bad to happen cos he thinks nobody would dare.

Sully's like the tom in the lorry park. He's laid out so many opps in his career, starting with Kamale and Lee Greene and going right up to Dris and Jamie, not to mention the Irish. I shouldn't be saying this even though everyone knows. But circumstances have changed. Sully is sitting across the table from me and he's telling me that maybe I'll live and maybe I'll die. And cos he's the top boy and he's in his ends, he's in his top boy office, of course he's relaxed. He ain't afraid cos he thinks nobody would dare.

I lean back in the green plastic chair and I feel the pressure of the Glock on my back.

The way I would do it is I would thank Sully politely for seeing me and I'd say I was going to get his grub. Then as I was getting to my feet, I'd slowly reach behind for the Glock – no sudden movements – and I'd shoot him dead right there.

I look around. There's no CCTV in the Number One Caff. There's only one customer and he ain't paying us no attention. The staff know me, but they know better than to talk to the feds.

I look at Sully.

'I 'preciate you taking the time,' I say. 'I'll get the grub. You'll have it tonight.'

'If I don't get it, you know what happens next,' he says.

I get slowly to my feet. No sudden movements.

Sully looks at me and I look back at him.

'Well?' he says.

I can't do it.

'What are you waiting for?' he says with a frown.

I can't do it.

'Nothing,' I say.

I turn and go.

I cross the road back to the car park. I need to think of somewhere to do the handover. Somewhere there'll be people. Where I'll be safe.

I look at my phones.

It's going long on Summerhouse. There's fire.

THE TOM IN THE LORRY PARK

While I'm spending the day dodging Sully and Dushane and running for my life, Mandy is on the estate organising a protest against the evictions. Even if I didn't have the issue I have, I wouldn't go to the protest. Apart from drug dealers shouldn't put themselves in situations like protests, why fight a battle that's already lost? Jeffrey and the developers – who include Dushane, even though he keeps that very quiet – have won, innit? Maybe not Jeffrey, on account of him being dead. But the developers, they have definitely won. Once the last few families have been thrown out, the bulldozers will go in. No protest is gonna stop that.

Turns out the bailiffs came early in the morning to throw out this Indian family, Mrs Khatri and her kids, and Mandy and Ralph and them did all they could to obstruct the bailiffs and make life difficult for them.

A couple of kids were playing football and keepie uppies on the access road, out of the way of the protest in the actual estate, when suddenly Dushane comes flying past.

The feds are after him. He disappears into Summerhouse, where the feds are always a little nervous about entering unless they're mobbed up. This cop car comes screeching round the corner and runs into the kids. Everyone's on their socials about it with all different versions. Some are saying two kids were hit. Some are saying it's three. And one of them at least is dead.

That was what done it.

As soon as word spreads about the feds killing the kid, people start pouring out of their flats and joining the protest and shouting at the police. More people arrive from outside the estate. Soon they're throwing Molotov cocktails at the feds. Someone sends out a photo on social media of a police car on fire in the courtyard.

It's a fucking full-scale riot. It's like the London riots when I was a kid. Like Broadwater or Brixton before I was born.

Apparently after the kid got killed the feds get outta the estate as fast as they can.

My phone rings. It's Kieron.

'Yo?'

'You seeing what's going on in Summerhouse?'

'Yeah, bruv. What the fuck?'

'The youth is outta control, bruv. My mum's worried that they're gonna come in and loot the house.'

'That ain't gonna happen, they know who lives there.'

'That's what I told her. Listen, bruv. Man called me, innit. He wants me to meet him. You know what that's about?'

'Nah,' I say. 'It's gonna be all cool. I went to the Number One Caff and talked to him. He weren't happy, but as long as I give him back his food it's all gonna get straightened out.'

'Yeah, he told me. He said your attitude's gotta be correct.'

'It will be.'

'Did he say anything about me?'

'Nah, man. All Sully wants is his bits back. This is on me. Nothing to do with you.'

'Glad to hear it, bruv, cos my mum is going down a bit more every day. I can see this ting is moving fast inside her now.'

'I got you, bro. Don't stress. I'm bringing man his food tonight.'

'He wants me there for it.'

'That's a good sign, right? Means he trusts you.'

'I hope so.'

'There's nothing to worry about. I'll see you there in a bit.'

'In a bit,' he says.

I call Becks.

'Jaq, I'm so relieved to hear your voice,' she says. 'Are you all right?'

'I'm fine.

'Have you heard about Summerhouse?'

'Yeah, it's a madness. Listen, babes. I just want you to know that I talked to Sully.'

'What did he say?'

'I'm giving him back his tings tonight.'

'Did he give you a pass?'

'Yeah,' I lie to her. 'It's all good.'

'Thank god,' she says. 'So it's all over?'

'It will be soon,' I tell her. 'It's gonna be OK.'

'Listen, my dad's driving me crazy. So what I'm going to do is take baby Jack and go to yours. That's OK, isn't it? If he's given you a pass?'

If I tell her don't go to mine, she'll be suspicious. And also, if I make it out of Summerhouse alive, I want Becks to be waiting at home for me.

'Cool,' I say. 'I'll see you there.'

'Can't wait,' she says.

My next call is to Dushane. One of the bags belongs to him and I need to make sure he gets it back. Cos if I give both bags to Sully, Sully might end up keeping them. Dushane wouldn't blame him. He'd blame me, so even though I get a pass from Sully I'd still have Dushane to worry about. Even though he has this Jeffrey murder thing going on, I don't wanna take a risk with him.

He picks up straight off.

'It was me,' I say. 'I took the grub. I know I done wrong. But I'm trying to make it right. So I'm giving him his food back. That's why I'm calling you cos I know one of the bags is yours.'

'Where?' Man sounds tense. It's understandable. His name is all over the news and socials. Wanted by police for Jeffrey's murder.

'I'm lining that up now,' I say.

'It needs to be in Summerhouse.'

That could work, I'm thinking. There ain't gonna be no feds on the estate and there'll be a lotta people around, so it won't be easy for Sully to do anything I would prefer him not to do. People are saying they're setting up a perimeter, but Summerhouse is big and the feds can't control every entrance and exit.

'A'right,' I say.

'And make sure it's all man's fucking food, all of it.'

'It's all there,' I say. 'I ain't touched nothing.'

'Yeah, you better fucking not. Just text me where on this phone.'

'A'right,' I say and we hang up.

Next I call Sully and I tell him that Dushane says it has to be in Summerhouse. He ain't exactly pleased but at least he don't make a big deal of it. He wants to know where.

It comes to me. Somewhere where there'll be plenty of people.

'The community centre,' I say.

'When?'

'An hour,' I say.

I leave the car half a mile away from Summerhouse cos the feds are definitely going to be on high alert and stopping every Black driver they see. I take the two bags, but leave the Glock. This ain't the night to be caught carrying a strap. But it does mean that if things go wrong with Sully, I ain't got no defence.

Risk I have to take.

I shoulder the bags and head to Summerhouse, keeping off the main road and using the little alleys and streets. I know them like the back of my hand and the feds don't.

The closer I get to Summerhouse, the more sirens I hear. Police and fire brigades mostly, but also a few ambulances. Whatever's going on there now, there's casualties. I can smell smoke in the air.

When I arrive, there's feds all over but there ain't enough of them to keep people from slipping in and out, specially now it's dark, and I get through no problem. I text Dushane and Sully that I'm nearly there.

Once I'm in, I don't recognise the place, and I was born and raised here. There's smoke and there's fires. There's ballied-up youths running round all over the place. They're tearing the orange grilles off the doors and windows of the empty flats and breaking windows and starting fires. A big, old TV set comes crashing down from off one of the walkways. It could of killed someone but nobody seems to give a fuck. Up in the sky, the Hackney helicopter is buzzing over the estate, no doubt taking videos and pictures for evidence for when they get round to nicking people for this, which they will do soon as people get tired of rioting and go home to bed.

I keep a look out for Kieron. I'd feel safer if he was around. I ask a couple of people if they've seen him, but they ain't.

I head towards the community centre, ignoring all the youths who are running round creating havoc. There's cars on fire and windows getting smashed. I just want to give Dushane and Sully back their bits, get my pass and go home and get into bed with Becks and work out what the fuck the future holds for me. Cos I am done with the road. I don't want no more of this shit, this stress. If I can't get to sleep at night, I wanna be counting sheep and not top boy ghosts.

Assuming, that is, Sully gives me the pass. At least here in Summerhouse, I'm safe. He wouldn't do nothing in front of all these people who know me and who know him. You can talk to a couple of brothers and tell them not to say anything to the feds about who shot their older brother in the head. But you can't give that talk to a whole estate of people. Someone's not gonna get the message and they will give names.

Nah, if Sully wants to make me suffer, it won't be tonight.

I'm close to the community centre when suddenly Dushane comes up from behind. He's got his hoodie up and his head down.

'Got everything here?' he says, blocking my way.

'Yeah, it's all there,' I tell him.

'Give me the bags,' he says.

'What are you doing?'

'Give me the fucking bags,' he says, grabbing at them.

I would of given him his bag but he didn't give me the chance.

'Get your hands off me,' I shout at him.

He punches me in the face and I go down and bang my head on the pavement. He gives me another couple of digs, grabs the bags and runs off.

By the time I've got to my feet, he ain't nowhere in sight.

This is fucking not good. Sully ain't gonna like this. If he even believes me, which he might not. There's blood on my forehead. Maybe that's a good thing. Maybe it'll convince Sully I'm telling the truth.

I make my way through the madness to the community centre. The youth are running fully amok now, smashing everything they can get their hands on. The helicopter searchlight lands at random, lighting up one spot before moving on to another.

Inside, it's like a pit stop where people are using the toilets and there's food and drink being given out by Mandy and her friends. Sully is waiting and he don't look happy.

'So when do I wait around for you? Where the fuck is it?'

'Dushane just robbed all the fucking food. He just jumped me.'

'Jaq, don't fuck with me, you know.'

'I'm not.'

'You're a fucking liar.'

He shoves me in the chest and pushes me through the double doors into the little hallway entrance and throws me up against the wall.

'What are you talking about?' he shouts in my face. 'You think it's a game? Don't play with me.'

He slams the wall an inch from the side of my head with the palm of his hand. 'How did Dushane know you was gonna be here?'

'I wanted to be sure he would get his food so I wouldn't have to worry about him coming after me, innit.'

Sully stares at me with pure hatred. 'You ain't getting no pass,' he says.

I should of done him in the Number One Caff. Why the fuck didn't I lay him out when I had the chance?

Then he says, 'And Kieron didn't get a pass either.'

I can't believe what I'm hearing. It's like the world has stopped spinning cos I know exactly what he's saying with that.

Mandy comes hurrying in from the main hall. 'Jaq, are you all right?'

'This ain't got nothing to do with you,' Sully tells her.

'I wanna hear that from Jaq,' she says.

'Shut up,' Sully says. He looks outside at the chaos. 'And you accuse me of wrecking Summerhouse? You seen what your mob's doing out there?'

'They ain't my mob.'

'Nah, but you started this shit.'

'What started this shit was started a long time ago. Poverty and discrimination. Harassment and neglect. For generations. That's what started it. All you done was take advantage of it. What I done was to try and change it.'

She might as well be talking Chinese for all Sully cares. 'Have a nice day,' he says.

He slams me into the wall and marches outside, to find Dushane and the food, I'm assuming. The showdown that was always coming between them two is gonna happen tonight. Ain't no doubt about that.

'Jaq, are you all right?' Mandy says when he's gone.

'It's good. I'm calm,' I tell her. 'Was Kieron here?'

'Nah, I ain't seen him. What's happened?'

I know exactly what's happened. I call Kieron but there's no answer. I'm sick to my stomach. I turn to go.

'Don't go out there,' Mandy says. 'It ain't safe.'

I ignore her and make my way through the mob to Kieron's yard. The door's been repaired since Immigration bust it down that morning they came for Kieron. I knock. I'm praying that Kieron's gonna answer the door. That I'm wrong in what I'm thinking. Please be home, Kieron.

Please be home.

But Kieron ain't home.

Diana comes to the door. She's obviously worried.

'Jaq?' she says. She's surprised to see me.

'Is Kieron in?'

'No. I thought he was meeting you.'

And then I know it's all true. Kieron didn't get a pass. Kieron lied to cover up for me and now he's dead. Sully killed him and it's my fault.

As I'm walking away, Diana calls after me. I don't stop.

I don't wanna tell her that the son she loved, the son who looked after her all this time of her illness, is never coming home.

I hear a gunshot. I don't know who's fired or who's been shot. If it's Sully or Dushane. Jimmy once told me that enemies don't fall out. Friends fall out. Family fall out. And when they do, it's even more bitter and they make the worst enemies for each other. All that love turns to pure hate. Summerhouse is burning tonight, and in the smoke and the flames there are two men who used to love each other who are now trying to kill each other.

By the time I get to mine it's the small hours of the morning. I put my car keys on the kitchen top and I see Becks lying asleep on the sofa. For a minute, I think I'm looking at Lauryn.

'You're back?' she says, all sleepy. 'I was so worried.'

I drop onto the sofa beside her.

'Is everything going to be all right?' she asks.

'Everything's gonna be OK.'

'OK.'

She snuggles into me, her head on my chest, and breathes deeply.

'Good,' she says. 'Is it all over?'

'Yes,' I say. 'It's all over. We're safe now.'

She squeezes my hand. 'We can start looking for the cottage,' she says.

I feel guilty for lying to her, but I go along with playing happy families. 'And the dogs.'

'I don't like small dogs,' she says. 'I like Labs and Golden Retrievers and collies.'

'We'll get one of each.'

She laughs and kisses me. 'I'm so relieved this is all over.'

But it ain't over. Depending who comes out of Summerhouse alive, Dushane or Sully, there's still something I'm gonna have to do.

LAURYN'S FUNERAL

Dushane wasn't the top boy he was back in the day. Plus, because of the Jeffrey murder and the feds being after him, he was desperate. And you don't make good choices when you're desperate. My money was on Sully.

And I was right.

They found Dushane's body the next morning in this courtyard near Summerhouse. He'd been shot. Everyone has a theory. Everyone thinks they know what went down. I wasn't there, obviously, but personally I don't think there's any doubt that it was Sully who laid Dushane out. I talked to Bradders and Samsi about it in the hospital where Bradders was after Dushane shot him as he was running from Sully. They said Sully and Junior were chasing after Dushane, who was carrying two bags with fifteen kilos in each bag. That'll slow a man down. Maybe if Dushane had dropped the food and all that weight he might of got away. But man was never gonna drop his grub. Without it, Dushane was nothing. And with it, he was dead.

Even though the night of the riot kind of seemed at the

time like the end of the world as we know it, next morning people just get up and go about their business. People have to go to work. Kids have to go to school. Tash, Sully's daughter, has to go to school. And, as usual, Sully picks her up from her mum's and takes her. According to the rumours, Sully is cutting through the park after dropping Tash off when someone comes up behind him. It's Stef, and Stef has a gun.

No one knows exactly how it happened. Maybe Sully talked him out of it, maybe Stef didn't have the balls. But Sully didn't die. He walks on to where he's left his car. He gets inside. The alpha male. The tom cat in the lorry park. He's got his food back and he's seen off another of his enemies no problem, his brother rival Dushane. He's chilled.

He's reaching for his seat belt when someone casually walks past and fires a single shot into his head.

Sully slumps on the steering wheel, right on the horn. It blares for an hour before anyone takes any notice. Sully wasn't afraid of anything. He had no reason to be. He had no enemies left standing. So he believed.

There's a lotta speculation about who laid him out. One name in the mix is Stef, which is possible. He might of got his nerve back up after whatever happened in the park with Sully, then followed him to the car. Si's name also gets mentioned, but no one seriously thinks Si had the balls to go up against Sully.

Junior's name is also in there, kind of a surprise. But some people think that with Dushane outta the way Junior saw an opening for a new top boy and he took it with both hands.

Then there's the Irish. The mandem are talking about

how some of Jonny's cousins came over from Dublin and took their revenge. Jonny was a name over there in Ireland and he had friends. I don't buy that one, though. I ain't seen or heard of the Irish round the ends since that day in the old people's home when Sully and Dushane paid them an unexpected visit.

One name that people ain't talking about is Jimmy the Indian. Cos no one knows that I talked to Jimmy about the problem I was having with Sully. Yeah, it could of been Jimmy. Him doing me a favour for Violet – I still can't get my head round him and Mum being together, I can't lie. It could of been Jimmy. It's the way he would of done it. Quiet and sneaky. But job done, innit.

My name is in the mix. I've told you enough times I don't say names out loud when I'm talking about this kind of thing, and specially not my own name. So obviously out loud I ain't gonna say nothing. I ain't gonna admit to killing Sully, innit. Are you mad? But, can't lie, everyone knows Kieron was my guy and Sully laid him out when he didn't have no good reason to. And – just think this through – if Sully killed Kieron like he did, for basically fuck all, sooner or later he was gonna come after me cos I done a whole lot more. He was coming, no doubt about that. So the question is, am I just gonna sit back and wait? Am I? Seriously? I'm saying out loud it weren't me and you can take that whatever way you want.

The feds, being generally fucking useless and corrupt, ain't got no idea, and they never will. So maybe we'll never know for certain who laid out Sully.

Over the next few weeks there's a lotta funerals in Summerhouse. I go to all of them. Kieron's is sad. His mum Diana is so sick that she's in a wheelchair. Mandy and Ralph take turns to push her. I cry all the way through the service, wishing how I'd never told him I'd taken the food.

It ain't a big crowd for Lauryn at the crematorium chapel, to say the least. Mandy and Ralph from Summerhouse, and Shelley and Naomi from the nail bar, and Bradders, Samsi and Romy from the road, they're here. Becks is with me, obviously, holding my hand. I thought we should bring baby Jack, but Becks said funerals were no place for babies and we got a girl from Summerhouse to mind him.

'My dad's gonna be late,' I say, turning to look at the door.

'I know,' she says, squeezing my hand. 'I know.'

'Where is he?'

'He'll be here soon, I'm sure,' she says.

The service is just about to start when the door opens. My heart jumps into my mouth. Jimmy the Indian comes in, alone. He's wearing a beautiful black suit and white shirt and black tie. The crease in his trousers is so sharp he could cut someone with it.

He comes up in the front row and leans to whisper in my ear. 'Your dad's hurt his back. It's a slipped disc. He's in agony and he can't travel. He's so sorry. He sends his love.'

'It's a'right. I knew he wouldn't come,' I say.

'Violet can't come either,' he says. 'She's just too upset.'

The only surprise would of been if Mum had come. Jimmy makes his face all sympathetic, pats my arm and goes and takes a seat.

The crematorium gives every funeral a thirty-minute slot. You get half an hour to say goodbye, but we're done in less than twenty. Shelley makes a nice speech, but no one has much to say about Lauryn.

We say our goodbyes and file out. There's hugs and condolences, but I'm just numb. I want it to be over. Jimmy suggests we all go to the pub and have a few drinks, but no one's really up for it. He gives me one of his big hugs and says to give baby Jack a kiss from him. He goes off with a sad smile.

'What the fuck?' I say to Becks as we come up to the car.

There's two white people waiting by it. I ain't ever seen the fella before. The woman is Sharon.

'What the fuck are you doing here?' I say to her. 'Show some fucking respect.'

'We have to talk to you about something,' the fella says. He's full of cop attitude. A smirking bully.

'No, you don't,' I say. 'Get out of my way.'

'Becks,' Sharon says, 'I've been trying to get hold of Jaq for a long time and this is the only place I knew she'd be for certain. It's up to you whether you want to hear this or not?'

'Give me a minute, babes,' I say to Becks.

'Are you sure?' she says.

'I'm calm.'

Becks goes and sits on a bench where she can see us but can't hear us.

'You fucked us, Jaq,' the fella says. 'We had it all lined up, but you went and let us down.'

'Yeah, well. Shit happens, things change. You know what I mean? We move on.'

'No, we don't move on. This was a big deal for us. And you need to make it right.'

‘You can fuck off,’ I tell him. ‘There’s nothing I need to make right for you.’

‘That’s where you’re wrong, Jaq,’ Sharon says. ‘You need to play ball with us on this one. Cos if you don’t, we will fuck you right up.’

I stare at Sharon. I’m this close to punching her out.

The fella says, ‘I advise you to listen very carefully to what I’m telling you. A murder investigation team is being put together as we speak. There’s going to be thirty detectives looking into every unsolved murder committed by the Summerhouse gang, going back at least ten years. All it takes is a phone call and your name is at the top of the MIT’s list of persons of interest.’

‘You ain’t scaring me,’ I say.

‘You should be scared,’ he says. ‘Because they will go through your life with a fine tooth comb. You will have detectives crawling all over you. It will be a deep investigation. If you’ve ever even crossed a crossing when the light’s been red, they will find out about it. Is that what you want?’

No, it is not what I want.

‘It doesn’t have to be that way,’ Sharon says. ‘We’re offering you something here and you’d be stupid not to take it.’

‘I ain’t robbing man if that’s what you’re thinking,’ I tell them.

‘It’s a lot easier than that,’ the fella says.

I could tell them to fuck off, but I don’t want the feds all over my life. I’ve always been careful hiding my tracks, but if they really come after me, they might find something I’ve overlooked. Or someone might talk. I don’t wanna take that chance.

'What is it?' I ask.

Sharon and the fella look at each other, like who's gonna tell her? In the end it's the fella who speaks.

'Sharon and I are having a problem with a colleague at work,' he says.

What the fuck?

'This colleague, she's putting our careers, our lives, in danger.'

'Did she find out about the Dickie Simms thing? Is that what you're telling me?'

'She suspects something,' Sharon says. 'We need to stop her before she reports it.'

'Stop her how?' I say.

They share another look. I know exactly what they have in mind.

'Listen,' I say, 'if you wanna stop her, go ahead.'

'We need alibis,' the fella says. 'It needs to be someone else.'

'It needs to be you,' Sharon says.

'Wait? You want me to stop this person?'

'We want you to take care of her,' Sharon says. 'Permanently.'

'Do this for us and we'll make sure the MIT never gets your name,' the fella says.

Mandy and Ralph pass on the way to their car. They both wave. Mandy looks concerned. Romy, Bradders and Samsi don't like the look of who I'm talking to and they don't say nothing as they go past.

I go over to Becks on the bench. 'Let's go, babes,' I say.

'Is everything all right?' she asks.

I would like a life where Becks don't have to ask me every day if everything's all right. At least that's what I tell myself. When I feel the pressure's getting too much my mind always goes to the vision of the cottage with the dogs where we have baby Jack and the baby that these days Becks is talking about wanting more and more.

But Sharon and her friend want me to kill a fed.

I know myself. I know that if I really wanted the cottage life I would take steps to make it happen, which I haven't done, and, I can't lie, I ain't got any plans to do any time soon. Maybe the cottage dream is the weak part of me. It's definitely where I go when I get scared. But I know once I've had time to process this shit with Sharon I'll figure out a way to deal with it.

I can handle Sharon.

That's the strong part of me.

ACKNOWLEDGEMENTS

Top Boy started life as a four-part television series. It first aired on Channel 4 in 2011, and it has just finished its fifth and final season on Netflix. During that time many, many creative debts have built up. It is my pleasure to acknowledge them.

My brother Gerry Jackson first introduced me to the world of Jaq, Dushane, Sully, Kieron, Lauryn and the mandem. Without Gerry there would never have been a *Top Boy*.

Charles Collier is a brilliant agent with strategic vision for his clients. In 2009 he put me together with producers Charles Steel and Aly Flind of Cowboy Films. Charles and Aly have been supportive throughout our long collaboration, pitching ideas and persuading me to rethink some of mine if they thought they weren't working. More than anyone they were responsible for getting the scripts to the screen.

Drake and Future and their team at DreamCrew, and LeBron James and Maverick Carter's SpringHill outfit, were instrumental in *Top Boy*'s resurrection after it was dropped by Channel 4. Without them, *Top Boy* would not have had its Netflix incarnation.

At various stages, Elliott Swift, Daniel West, Tyrone Rashard, Verona Rose and Elliot Warren were part of the writers' room. The sessions were intense, but always fun. They were a pleasure to work with.

Ashley Walters and Kane Robinson took the characters of Dushane and Sully and made them their own, adding further layers and psychological depth. They are exceptional actors, as is rapper Santan Dave, David Omoregie.

While Season 3 was in development a young fan asked me pointedly why there were no gay women in *Top Boy*. Jaq was the result. She was not intended to be a leading character. But the rushes revealed the astonishing screen presence of Jasmine Jobson, and I quickly revised the scripts.

Simbiatu Ajikawo, Saffron Hocking, Adwoa Aboah, Shone Romulus, Kadeem Ramsey, Howard Charles, Letitia Wright and Nicholas Pinnock are just some of the many spellbinding actors who have helped populate the *Top Boy* world. There isn't space to acknowledge the entire cast, but there is imdb.com.

It's no surprise that *Top Boy* was so perfectly cast. Des Hamilton and his superb team brought us outrageously talented young newcomers like Micheal Ward, Araloyin Oshunremi, Joshua Blisset, Malcolm Kamulete, Xavien Russell, Hope Ikpoku and the heart-breaking Ricky Smart, as well as finding perfect matches for our older characters in established actors like Sharon Duncan-Brewster, Ashley Thomas, Joséphine de La Baume, Lisa Dwan, David Hayman, Marsha Millar, Hugo Silva and Benedict Wong.

Yann Demange directed Season 1 and set the tone for

the series. Jonathan van Tulleken, Brady Hood, Myriam Raja, Nia DaCosta, Koby Adom, William Stefan Smith and Aneil Karia followed in Yann's wake, each bringing their own talents and sensibilities to the episodes they directed. My friend Reinaldo Marcus Green took the show to new heights when he kicked off the first Netflix season.

Behind every director there is, often literally, a director of photography. We have been lucky to have Chris Ross, Tat Radcliffe, Rina Young and Kanamé Onoyama, among others.

And behind the actors, directors and cinematographers there have been armies of talented and hardworking people up at dawn and out in all weathers. I am grateful to all of them: runners, unit drivers, location managers, production designers, set decs, caterers, costume designers, assistant directors, prop masters, gaffers, sound editors, hair and make-up artists, colourists and everyone in the various production offices over the years.

Music supervisors Abi Leland, Toby Williams and Ed Bailie, among others, have given *Top Boy* a unique sound, along with composer Michael Asante. The legendary Brian Eno contributed a Bafta-winning score.

Jay Hunt greenlit *Top Boy* at Channel 4 long before Black Lives Matter and the Me Too movement. It took vision and courage to make a show with a ninety per cent Black cast and no stars. When Netflix picked up the show, Tara Duncan, Layne Eskridge, Aria Moffly, Ernest McNealey, Anne Mensah and Alice Pearse could not have been more supportive, and Aaron Lynch and Kate Bain worked tirelessly to make sure the show got out in front of the public.

Every line in this book owes something to everyone who has been involved in the show.

The novel itself would not exist if it were not for Jamie Byng and his infectious enthusiasm. When Jamie asked me to lunch to discuss the possibility of a *Top Boy* novel, I walked into the restaurant to tell him I was sorry but I couldn't see a way to do it. By the time I left I had agreed to write it. It had been fifteen years since my last novel, and David Godwin, my literary agent, probably doubted that I would ever write another. If so, he never said anything. David has always been encouraging, supportive, humorous and calm.

Finally, I want to thank Ellah Wakatama for her sensitive and diligent editing.